CHRISTMAS MURDER ON THE SLOPES

Totally Addictive Cozy Mystery

Massachusetts Cozy Mysteries
Book 7

ANDREA KRESS

© 2024 ANDREA KRESS

Chapter 1

A cold December Saturday found the two couples—Amanda and fiancé Brendan and her sister Louisa and boyfriend Rob—having a leisurely lunch at Catalano's in Boston's North End. It was a sentimental choice for a midday meal as it was the place where much of the courting of Amanda Burnside and the dashing police detective had taken place. Mr. Russo, the proprietor, thought it appropriate to take ownership in having facilitated the relationship with his excellent cuisine although that was only a small part of its evolution.

It had been a busy week for Amanda, a private investigator working mostly with her father's law firm, as well as for Brendan, supervisor of detectives in the Boston Police Department, and for Louisa, a designer in the prestigious Monsieur Josef Dress Salon. Only Rob, owner of the Oasis nightclub, was truly taking a day off work as they finalized their plans for a ski holiday in the Berkshires, funded by a reward from Amanda's last case.

"Our cousin Aggie and her husband, John, are insistent that we stay with them. I'm reluctant to decline so as not to hurt their feelings," Amanda began. "They are such lovely people."

"I bet you say that about all our family members," Louisa said with a smile. "I haven't been there, but I got the impression their home was small. And we agreed that we would stay at the Mountain Aire, remember? Aggie said it was *the* place to stay, not just by reputation, but because it's so close to the ski resort."

"Their home is not small. There's room for us all. I just don't want to create more work for them. On the other hand, her feelings might be hurt if we don't stay."

"Let's add one more room to the reservation at the hotel so they'll be there with us," Rob suggested. "It will also be a break from cooking and entertaining us."

Amanda hesitated. "How about this compromise. We stay tomorrow night with them. And then we all go to the Mountain Aire for the rest of the trip? I know Aggie is anxious for us all to see their house. After John being a bachelor, she has spiffed up the place with curtains and cushions, all the things a single man doesn't think about."

"I hope you're not including my place in your broad assessment," Brendan said, his blue eyes twinkling.

"You must admit it's rather sparse."

"It's basic. It's simple. It suits my needs. After we get married next year, you can spruce it up any way you like. Just not too many ruffles and bows."

"I certainly hope not," Louisa said. "For those of you who have been asleep this past decade, the trend is a streamlined look: glass, steel, bold. Art Deco. In case you hadn't noticed, we've been moving away from the fussy, frilly look."

Amanda bowed her head to what she considered her younger sister's superior sense of design and fashion and continued, "I'm sure Aggie will want to show off her newly acquired domestic skills."

"Do you mean that she already has planned a big meal? And the rooms are already made up?" Brendan asked.

"Exactly. She called yesterday and told me. We don't want to show her up by zooming off to a fancy hotel instead. That way, we'll have done our family duty as well as providing them with a respite. Being a doctor in rural West Adams with another office in Pittsfield makes for a busy life for the both of them."

"Done. I'll call the hotel as soon as we've finished lunch," Rob offered.

"Thank you so much," Amanda said.

Mr. Russo came to the table with a breadbasket full of focaccia and two plates, one of olive oil and the other butter, as he knew that Americans couldn't seem to eat bread without it. They were already enjoying red wine and only had to utter their selection of entrées before resuming their conversation.

"I hope you'll enjoy some time off for a change," Louisa said to Brendan.

"I'm looking forward to the vacation, but I confess that I'm a bit apprehensive as I've never skied before. It looks positively dangerous," he replied.

"Said the man who apprehends bad people," Amanda said. "You'll take to it in no time. You just point your skis in the right direction and gravity does the rest."

Brendan looked at her to see if she were joking, but she was serious.

"Really. Even little children ski."

"Thank you for adding to my discomfort. Children have no fear. I've got farther to fall and more to break than any youngster."

"There's always an instructor there, so you can take lessons," Louisa said.

"If you get too cold or wet, the clubhouse has a bar and a roaring fire going at all times," Amanda said.

"This is beginning to sound better," Brendan said.

"Speaking of cold places, there is a new Russian restaurant in town. One of our clientele was raving about the caviar there," Louisa said as she patted her blonde hair back into place.

"Gosh, the people in that country have been through such hard times—do they even have a cuisine any longer?" Amanda asked.

"Fancy restaurants are not part of the new order in Russia," Rob said. "This place is meant to be an homage to the days of the Empire. The food is quite good. And, naturally, they have a man in full costume playing a balalaika."

"It's 1933. Not only has the old empire been gone for more than fifteen years, but the only people who could afford to eat caviar in the first place were a small percentage of the population. The folks at the top," Brendan said.

"I don't think the owner of the New Metropol was one of the aristocracy, even though he suggests that he was the illegitimate son of some prince. He's just providing an illusion that everyone likes to indulge in. Vast palaces, troikas with their bells coursing along snowy streets, enormous ballrooms and banquets. And none of those pesky serfs," Rob said.

"So, no potatoes," Amanda observed.

"Oh, yes, potatoes, but elegantly presented in cream sauce."

"Those poor people," Amanda said. "The regular folk, I mean," she added. "We don't hear much about them, which makes me think things must be bad for the ordinary people."

"As it always goes," Rob said. "And whoever the new folks in power are, you can bet the common folk won't be much better off. No matter what they're being told. But there is a group of immigrants from Russia who call themselves émigrés, to distinguish themselves from the lower classes. These people pass themselves off as aristocrats who have been deprived of their birthright and have been forced to live in reduced circumstances, sponging off their American acquaintances who are more than happy to brag of the honor. The next thing you know, one of them will claim to be one of the missing Romanovs."

"But I thought all of them were killed," Amanda said.

"There are varying reports of what happened—but who knows?" Rob said.

"How do you know so much about all this?" Amanda asked.

"You'd be surprised what you overhear from the tables at the Oasis. There's an older man who comes in by himself. I have no idea how he came upon us in the first place, but it seems we're sort of a refuge for him. He comes in early and sits at our small bar and chats with the bartender. One of these Russian women seems to have made herself a permanent fixture in his home, invited by his wife who, of course, thinks it is a great privilege to host her presence. He says she acts as if all the household should be at her beck and call and treats him as if he were the butler."

"Poor man," Louisa said with a wry smile. "I can't imagine Mother getting into a situation like that."

Louisa was correct about that. But there were other women who were not so discerning. And it was all to come to a head during what was supposed to be a relaxing ski trip.

Chapter 2

It was quite a production getting the ski equipment secured to the roof of Rob's spacious sedan as well as the luggage, boots and outdoor clothing crammed into the trunk.

"It might have worked better to have taken one of your trucks," Louisa said, referring to the vehicles that transported the barrels of beer and crates of alcohol to the Oasis.

"In that event, there might even have been enough room for your entire wardrobe," Amanda said.

"But there's only room in the cab of the truck for three people. We'd have to draw straws to decide who would be the lonely person in the dark in the back," Rob said.

"That's a horrid image. Rolling around with the luggage with each twist and turn of the roadway," Louisa said with a shiver. "Brendan, where did you get your skis?"

"I rented them. It seemed like the sensible thing to do. If I take to skiing or it takes to me, I'll consider buying some in the future. After a hefty pay raise, that is."

Once everything had been tied down, they left the Burnside house with the girls' parents waving from the open front door. While initially apprehensive about the two unmarried couples spending a holiday together, they were assured by Amanda that they would have separate sleeping quarters.

"Our best to Aggie and John!" Mrs. Burnside called out as they watched the car pull away.

Route 20 was the road to take west to Pittsfield, and they began by wending their way through Boston and crossing the Charles River at the Beacon Street Bridge. At that point, they were in the suburbs and, as most car commuter traffic had already passed in the other direction, it was smooth sailing on a nearly empty road.

Rob turned on the car's radio to listen to music for as long as they got a signal from Boston, and the Christmas songs made for a true holiday feeling. The road went through suburbs, then farmland and forests and became the main street or business section when they came to any town of note. There was no way to bypass the towns and the slower local traffic, but it gave them a chance to observe small town life in their home state, along with the industries that supported it.

They had agreed to stop in Springfield for lunch, which would leave them with a short drive to West Adams arriving in the early afternoon. They drove in view of the factories along the Connecticut River, through the downtown with its Gothic sandstone buildings and back out into the near suburbs, stopping at The Colonial Inn.

"It's darling!" Louisa exclaimed, almost leaping out of the car before Rob had pulled it to a full stop.

"Hardly Art Deco," Amanda commented.

The white, two-story, clapboard building had an expansive porch that likely had Adirondack chairs arranged facing the street in warmer weather. The columns were decorated in twining pine boughs and the front door sported an enormous Christmas wreath. The sign on the snowy front lawn declared that it was established in 1775 and was 'Springfield's Oldest Inn.'

Louisa put her arm through Rob's as they made their way across the cleared slate walk to the entrance, opened by a woman in period dress with a mobcap on her head. Louisa gasped as they were led into the foyer where they hung up their outerwear on a row of hooks next to period wallpaper and prints on the wall. Beyond a set of double doors that protected the room from the outside cold lay the main dining room. While everything inside spoke to the Early American period, many in the mix were probably reproductions. The woman led them to a table next to windows overlooking what must have been an extensive lawn, border shrubs and tall trees, now covered in snow. A fire had been lit and provided warmth and a homey scent.

"Gosh, this is beautiful," Louisa said. "Wouldn't it be wonderful to decorate a modern home in this style?"

"I'm all for the style," Brendan said. "I just hope the food is more modern. I'd rather not eat johnny cakes with watered-down ale."

"What are johnny cakes, anyway?"

"Some kind of cornmeal pancakes. I read that soldiers in that era would mix cornmeal with water, twirl a stick in it and cook it over a fire," he replied.

"Oh, yum," Amanda said, grimacing. "With the extra seasoning of tree bark."

"I think it's meant to be a soldier's food when on the march."

"I'm going to have the clam chowder. I bet Aggie will have some feast prepared and I don't want to disappoint her with a puny appetite," Amanda said.

The others were quiet as they perused the menu, each deciding quickly what they would have. Rob folded his menu and put it on the table.

"Tell me about Aggie and John," Brendan said as the waitress brought a carafe of hot coffee to the table. "I only met her that once."

"Aggie and I are the same age. Our fathers are brothers."

"And the girls could pass for twins," Rob added.

"She's a thoroughly good egg. She trained as a nurse in New York and after a job at the hospital fell through, she found out through a friend, Glenda, who grew up in West Adams, that the doctor there was looking for a temporary, part-time nurse for his practice. She thought it would be a short stint and she'd return to the City at the end of the summer. In the meantime, the doctor acquired the practice of a Pittsfield colleague who was retiring and suddenly he needed a full-time nurse. And as these things happen, romance blossomed."[1]

---

1. See MURDER AT HIGHFIELDS to get the whole story.

"That's a nice tale," Brendan said.

"He's a wonderful man, big and outdoorsy. Grew up somewhere out West."

"I don't think I could live in a small town the way they do. Where everybody probably knows your business and there isn't much to do," Louisa said. "And I certainly couldn't have a thriving fashion design career there. I'm glad I'm in Boston."

"No, you probably wouldn't enjoy living there, but she said it has its charms. Their next-door neighbor is the elderly Miss Manley, whom you met at Louisa's coming-out ball. At her house she has a regular tea gathering with her circle of women friends who share notes on who is doing what."

"Gossip, you mean," Brendan said.

"Yes, but very informative, I'll bet. Rob, just as you said you pick up all kinds of tidbits overhearing conversations at the Oasis, their tea group serves the same purpose."

"Except in our case, when alcohol is involved, people tend to lose their inhibitions more readily," Rob said.

After the waitress had returned and taken their orders, the talk returned to business.

"What's going on at the police department, Brendan?" Rob asked.

"That officer who was gifted to us by the Chicago Police Department turned out to be an asset after all. He's putting together a whole team of specialists to assist in the technical side of things."

"I thought you had folks who did that already."

"We had some people who could do fingerprint dusting and other rudimentary things, but he has actually reached out to an anthropologist at Harvard to come in as needed to help identify deceased victims."

"Please, Brendan. Not at the table," Louisa said.

Amanda laughed. "Now you sound just like Mother. 'Can't we talk about something more pleasant?'"

"I apologize," Brendan said. "I should have chosen my words more carefully." He stopped for a moment to collect his thoughts. "He has also gathered other people with forensic knowledge of the human body and those with ballistic experience."

Louisa gave him a puzzled look.

"See, sometimes using more pleasant terms only makes things less clear," Amanda said. "Look, here comes my soup. I hope you don't mind if I start."

ON THEIR WAY AGAIN, they headed northwest through the heavily wooded countryside, interrupted by small towns as the roadway became more winding.

"I've don't remember ever being here," Louisa said. "Have we been?" she asked her sister.

"Mother and Daddy took us on a vacation when we were both little and I don't remember much except expecting to see a bear and being greatly disappointed. We usually spent summers at the beach house in Maine," she explained to Brendan. "When the weather gets warmer, you'll have to come up."

"Beach houses are made for families who can be gone from their usual homes for several months," he reminded her.

"We'd all go up and Daddy would go back to Boston after the weekend. It was kind of fun being out in the woods up from the bay and walking into town for a change of pace," she said. "Not too bad a drive leaving early on Friday afternoon. The anticipation of smelling that first blast of wind from the sea was everything."

They slowed down as they approached more traffic in Lee, which was lined with two-story brick buildings housing shops and stores of every kind.

"See the lampposts?" Amanda asked, leaning forward to Louisa in the front seat. "In the summer they are hung with baskets of blooming flowers. Aggie sent me a postcard."

That got the expected noise of approval from her sister. "Now it's holly and pine boughs."

"There's a wonderful restaurant in Stockbridge, dating from colonial times, not too far from here. The Red Lion Inn," Amanda said.

"Not on our route today, but perhaps on the way back," Rob said. "We're not too far from Pittsfield and then onward to Utopia."

They left Lee and were briefly in open country before entering Lenox, which elicited more pleasant comments. "It's so quaint!"

"Brutal in a snowstorm, I imagine," Brendan said.

"We missed the turning of the leaves. I bet that's spectacular," Louisa said. Her head turned from side to side to take in everything, and she pointed to the impressive buildings on the main street.

Out in the country again as they headed toward Pittsfield the density of houses and farms along the road increased until they entered the city itself.

"I had no idea it was so big," Louisa said. "It's impressive that John has a practice here as well as West Adams." They passed government buildings, banks and storefronts and noticed a sign for a hospital. "That's where they'll take you after you break your leg, Brendan," she said with a giggle.

"Not funny. I can understand that skis were probably invented to get around in the snow. What I can't imagine is having those long, slim pieces of lumber tied to my boots and having to make my way down a hill and calling it fun."

"Mountain," Amanda corrected.

Brendan looked at her without expression. "And how do you get up to the top, anyway?"

"We used to have to sidestep up." She motioned with her hands.

"You're joking. All that effort to get to the top just to hurtle down to the bottom."

"I'm not joking. But now they have a motorized tow rope with handles that you grab on to, and it pulls you upward. Much less exhausting." Amanda looked over at him for a reaction.

"I wish I had been better informed before I agreed to this trip," Brendan said with only a hint of humor.

Once out of the city, they turned off toward West Adams and found themselves surrounded by forest intermittently cleared for farmsteads. The road was winding with icy places in spots, but mostly clear from the activity of previous traffic.

"Here we are," Louisa said, spotting the sign announcing they were entering the town of West Adams. She leaned forward to get the best view of the small town, with clumps of snow at the curbs from a prior plowing making access paths to the stores that lined the main street.

"There's a dress shop, Louisa. See, you could set up here just fine," Amanda teased.

"I'll bet all anyone wears here are flannel shirts and wool hats with ear flaps," she answered.

"Properly draped with sequins and feathers, a wool hat could look very chic. You could start a new trend in rural fashion."

Louisa ignored her sister. "What is the address again?"

"Aggie said once out of the business district to look for the lamppost on the left side

of the street, some high hedges and we'll see a doctor's shingle. There!"

"Which is their driveway?" Rob asked.

"I don't know. Let's just park on the street and go in."

They piled out of the car, surprised to see that few of the sidewalks into town had been shoveled although the path to the doctor's office had been cleared. Louisa had not changed into casual clothes that morning and picked her way along in her ankle high boots with the fur trim, holding onto Rob's arm in case she slipped and fell. Amanda was glad to be wearing lined wool pants although she could still feel the cold wind. They went up to the door and, opening it, set off a tinkling bell, letting anyone in the house know that someone was in the lobby of the doctor's home office. A door at the opposite end of the room was ajar and Aggie's head topped with a nurse's cap emerged from the kitchen of the house.

"Hello!" she cried, rushing to embrace Amanda, then Louisa, and standing back to shake hands with Brendan and Rob. She smoothed out her white uniform over which she wore a navy wool cardigan.

"What's that fantastic smell?" Amanda asked, moving into the kitchen. "A turkey!"

John came into the kitchen from a door to the rest of the residential part of the home and, after greetings, there were overlapping conversations about where to park the car, how the office was technically still open and how their trip had been so far. In the midst of all this noise and chatter in the kitchen, the bell over the door to the outside jingled and everyone was quiet. A woman came in from the cold and stared at the group that had now migrated from the kitchen to the reception area.

"May I help you?" Aggie asked.

"Is the doctor in?" the woman asked with a bold demeanor, looking at each of the three men trying to ascertain which one it would be: the blond-haired man in a camel hair coat, the black-haired man in a dark brown overcoat or the tallest of the three with broad shoulders and brown hair. It was he who stepped forward and introduced himself.

"These are my houseguests," he explained in the event she

thought this was a crowded clinic. He ushered her into one of the examination rooms and closed the door.

"We must have been a sight," Amanda said in a whisper.

"I'll move the car," Rob said, and Brendan followed to help unload the luggage and equipment.

"And you can come back in through the front door," Aggie said.

"Are you done for the day?" Amanda asked her cousin.

"Almost. I was just checking on the turkey. There's coffee on the stove, cream and sugar on the table. Help yourselves. I'll see if John needs me." She closed the door to the kitchen and Amanda and Louisa went through the dining room toward the front door and hung up their coats.

"What a cozy place," Louisa said. Noticing the radiators lining the walls, she added, "Thank goodness they have central heating."

"Did you think we were going to have to chop our own wood?"

"The place could stand a little spiffing up," Louisa said in a whisper. It was her polite code word meaning that the décor was outdated.

Amanda sighed in exasperation. "It's not as if a country doctor hosts cocktail parties on a regular basis. In fact, I'm sure, due to his busy practice, their social life is somewhat limited."

"Oh, dear," Louisa said with a small frown. "Poor Aggie."

They heard the commotion of the two men coming up the front steps and opened the door to have them place the bags inside. Another trip and the skis and poles came in and were stacked in a corner opposite the coatrack. They stamped the snow off their feet and took off their coats.

"There's coffee in the kitchen," Louisa said, and they went there, grateful for the warm beverage as they stood near the hot stove.

Aggie came back in from the door connecting the kitchen to the reception area. "John doesn't need me. No comprehensive exam, it's just going to be a chat. Let me see what's going on in the oven," she said, excusing herself to open the door with a potholder.

"Smells divine," Brendan said.

"It's got another hour to go. John will be done soon. Let me show you to your rooms."

Aggie led a brisk pace through the dining room to the stairway to the second floor. "Your mother was very clear about the arrangements, as you might expect. Amanda, you and Louisa are in this room and Brendan and Rob down the hall."

Louisa gave a resigned look because she knew her parents wouldn't have agreed to the trip unless the couples had separate sleeping quarters. She knew the same would apply to their rooms at the Mountain Aire and that Amanda would insist upon it as well.

"Just like sleep-away camp," Louisa said, eying the two single beds on either side of a nightstand.

"Not at all. Don't you remember there were bunk beds, no central heating and no electric lights in the cabins."

"True. And we won't have to deal with the endless chattering of bunkmates when we need our sleep."

"I can supply the chatter if you like," Amanda said. "Let's take out the essentials for the evening," she added, swinging her suitcase onto the bed and clicking the latches open. "Aggie said there's only one bathroom upstairs, which we'll have to share, although there's got to be one in his office, too, in the event of overcrowding."

"Are you going to change for dinner?" Louisa asked since she was already in a dress.

"No, I'm roughing it in these," Amanda replied, looking down at her pants. "Just need to get out of these boots into shoes. I'm going to freshen up." She went to the hallway and saw the bathroom door near the entrance to the master bedroom.

Partially unpacked, boots exchanged for shoes, all four made their way back down to the kitchen.

"That was fast," Aggie said. "But let's not all gather in the kitchen. I'll never be able to get this meal together with you all in the way."

"We're here to help," Brendan said.

"Actually, there's not much to be done. I've trimmed down the menu to have more time to chat with you all. Sweet potatoes are in the oven, peas ready to heat up, cranberry sauce is on the table. Let's adjourn to the living room and have a drink."

"Without John?"

"You all can start. Brendan, I'm appointing you the bartender while I go upstairs and change. I'll show you the drinks cabinet." Having done so, she left them to their choice of alcohol and left the room.

"Just look at the variety," Brendan said. "Even if I'm the barkeep, you'll have to keep your orders simple. I'm not making any sidecars or Manhattans."

"Spoilsport," Louisa said. She pulled back a curtain and looked outside. "Gosh, it's getting dark already."

"If you want something fancy, Rob is the one to ask."

Rob responded by putting his hand to the side of his head. "I almost forgot. There's champagne in the trunk. I'd better get it before it freezes."

Greeted by cheers, he went out to his car to retrieve it.

"He's the man for me," Brendan said. "Where might I find the glasses?"

Amanda took Louisa back to the dining room and between them juggled six coupe glasses back to the living room. No sooner had Rob returned than Aggie came down the stairs, having changed into a wool skirt, sweater and tights instead of the white stockings she had worn in her role as nurse.

"What's this?" she asked, seeing Rob holding up two bottles of champagne, one in each hand. "Let's wait for John. I'll see how he's coming along," she said.

"She's a quick-change artist. Monsieur Josef would love her as a model. Some of the girls are so pokey that it holds up a showing," Louisa said.

"That gives you and Monsieur more time to butter up the customers, doesn't it?" Amanda asked.

They sat down waiting for their hostess to reappear, which she did with a tray of simple hors d'oeuvres.

"Aggie, you're amazing!" Amanda said, meaning every word. "How do you manage two practice locations, this big house and now hosting us?"

"Organization and speed. John has just finished, so let's get the party going," she said.

As if on cue, John came through the doorway into the living room as Rob popped the cork on the champagne to the delight of everyone.

Chapter 3

The discussion over dinner was catching up on news of those present and the family members who were not, interspersed with compliments about the delicious food.

"Aggie, I had no idea you were so accomplished!" Amanda said.

"We didn't have a cook growing up, so I learned early." Even though they were first cousins, their fathers had experienced different fortunes in life. Amanda's father had married into an established and wealthy Boston Brahmin family while Aggie's father had married a woman of more modest means and made their life in Westchester County, New York. Their living situation had become more precarious as he recovered from lung damage in the Great War and was unable to work full time. Those days were long behind them, but the frugal household continued without live-in servants or a cook, something of which Aggie wasn't the least bit ashamed.

"Amanda's learning to cook, too," Louisa said. "She knows how to make coffee now."

That got a chuckle from the group.

"I'd be careful about the pot calling the kettle black," Brendan observed. "Although I thought the soufflé dinner you two cooked up was rather good."

"I just may take cooking classes and surprise you all," Amanda said. "By the way, how is the Mountain Aire doing? I heard it changed hands."

"Yes, Cash Ridley grew bored with his new toy and the Fosters, George and his son Greg, who sold it to him, bought it back. It seems to be doing just fine—full in the summertime, lots of leaf peepers in the fall and a smaller but steady ski crowd in the winter."

"Good for them. Now I know you are putting us up tonight, but I've already reserved three rooms at the Mountain Aire tomorrow in the hope that you and John can join us."

Aggie looked to John and back to her cousin. "Oh, we couldn't."

"Yes, you could. You've already planned to be gone skiing for those days, so why drive back home each night? It would be such fun for us all to be together."

"Thank you so much, but we couldn't impose," John said.

"It's not an imposition at all. We're imposing on you here! I'd have absolutely no fun if it were just Louisa with me," Amanda said with a wink to her sister. That broke the stalemate, and the Taylors agreed to go to the hotel the next day.

"The food is just as good as I remembered it when Cash used to treat us, but the atmosphere is a bit strained. I think that since the family's great luck in regaining their hotel, there is friction between the father and son about keeping it the same or expanding or changing it somehow," Aggie said.

"I'm not talking out of school, but that young woman who came in earlier is one of the workers at the hotel. She had chilblains, if you can imagine. Too much exposure to the cold. They're working her as a maid and a waitress along with a skeleton staff. I think George Foster is trying to cut corners as much as possible as he is starting to reach retirement age," John said.

"It's a familiar story about what to do when there is a family business. The question of whether the next generation wants to continue it and, if they do, will they change it," Rob said. "I'm glad that José and I see eye to eye for the most part on the running of the Oasis and that we're not related, because he likes to pretend he's the silent partner although he's very much on the scene."

"He's fine letting you do most of the work," Louisa said.

"I don't mind. I can't imagine he would last a week having to put in the hours that I do. He is standing in for me these next few days while his wife, Caroline, and his mother-in-law are on holiday."

"Gosh, they seem to get around," Louisa said.

Aggie and John looked at each other and the conversation stopped.

She was the first one to speak. "I hate to burst your bubble, but as a matter of fact, they're at the Mountain Aire. I saw them here in town yesterday and Hextilda Browne can't wait to see you all."

"CAROLINE IS ALL RIGHT, but I can't stand her mother," Louisa said as she changed into pajamas in the room she was sharing with Amanda. "She's so unpredictable."

"That's where you're wrong. She is predictably unpredictable on purpose. She loves to be the center of attention, and what better way to accomplish that than start off saying one thing and then doing another?"

"That might be interesting at a social gathering, but it's not in real life when people are depending on you."

Amanda turned to look at her sister. "In what way?"

"She made all kinds of overtures to Monsieur Josef about ordering a trousseau for Fred's wife."

"What? For Valerie? That doesn't sound like the Fred Browne I know."

"I don't know what happened, but after seeing all the sketches and keeping us on the hook for a month, she decided that it was really Valerie's family that should do the ordering. Which, of course, they didn't follow through on with us because they had already assembled one."

"That's strange. Maybe there were crossed wires," Amanda said.

Louisa shook her finger at her sister. "Stop apologizing for the Brownes. Yes, I know that could be a logical explanation and you tend to look kindly on the faults of others, but really! To this day I can't believe you ever dated Fred, that dour skinflint."

Amanda burst out laughing and sat on her bed. "You're absolutely right. I can't believe it either!"

"At last, we agree on something!" Louisa said and started laughing until tears came to her eyes.

There was a discreet knock on the door and Aggie put her head around the opening.

"Is everything all right?"

"Come in," Amanda, who had gained control of herself, said. "We were just recounting my close call with Fred Browne and his bizarre family."

Aggie began to laugh and sat down next to her. "She really is something else. Do you know she even suggested using me as her inspiration for a character in one of her books?"

That released another round of laughter.

"A nurse in a corset and low-cut gown?" Louisa asked.

"Can you imagine? I think she might have been thinking of using my real name, too."

"What a boon to John's practice, don't you think?" Amanda asked. "When we see her tomorrow, I'll be sure to remind her."

"You do, and I'll tell her Amanda is a much better name than Agnes for a bodice ripper novel."

Amanda picked up her pillow and held it up threateningly. Aggie jumped to her feet.

"Night all!" she said, making a hasty exit and laughing as the pillow hit the back of the closing door.

DESPITE THE SIGN on Doctor Taylor's office door, the next day brought in four patients who apologized for disturbing his plans but nonetheless sought medical attention. All he could do was shrug his shoulders when he told Aggie, and she replied that their guests could occupy themselves with walking the short distance into town and picking up whatever they might have forgotten to pack. What was to be a quick trip turned into most of the morning as they explored the shops and the quaint library.

Back at the Taylors', the last patient was treated and a simple lunch of sandwiches was made while the bags, skis and equipment were packed back into Rob's car. John and Aggie were to travel separately, not just because of the need for their luggage but in the event that there was some medical emergency—even though he had arranged for coverage from a colleague—for

which he might need to drive back to town or to Pittsfield. Finally on the road after the meal, they embarked on the short ride for the Mountain Aire. The trip brought back fond memories for John and Aggie and both must have been having the same thought as they reached for each other's hand and smiled.

Their small caravan came down into the shallow valley, with the mountains behind and the curving drive in front of the entrance. The tennis courts to the back were covered in snow, their nets stored for the season and the surfaces not likely to be shoveled clear but left to melt in the spring. As they neared the entrance, the drive was flanked by arborvitae that had been pruned to conical shapes and encircled with strands of berries and popcorn.

"How sweet! They've decorated the trees with food for the birds," Aggie said. "You wouldn't think the staff had time to do all that. No wonder they're being worked to the bone."

"The volume of guests is down in the winter. Perhaps the Fosters can get along just fine with minimal staff. Look at the parking lot," John said, noticing the lack of vehicles. He stopped in front of the hotel to let Aggie out and unload the ski equipment.

"This is the one part of the sport that I'm not fond of—hauling everything around." He had unstrapped the skis from the roof of the car and, hoisting them over his shoulder, walked them to the front doors and placed the skis upright beside them. Aggie had already taken her bag from the trunk and walked it to the door before George Foster hurried out.

"Doctor Taylor! What a surprise. No, no. Let me get Tony to help you with that." He put his head back inside and yelled, "Tony! Where are you?"

Moments later a man in a uniform came rushing out the door.

Foster glared at him and said in a stage whisper, "Where have you been?"

"Please," the porter said, taking the bag from Aggie and bringing it inside. She followed in past the two large pine wreaths hanging on the front doors, through the foyer, into the warm interior of the Mountain Aire.

"It looks so festive," she said, noticing the fir tree in the corner decorated simply with paper chains and colored lights.

"We had a little party for the children from the West Adams school who came out to help decorate," George said.

"What a lovely idea," Aggie said, walking closer. She saw pine cones hanging from strings, thin slices of orange that were drying out and small bunches of cinnamon sticks tied with red ribbon nestled within the branches. "And it smells divine, too."

"Mrs. Taylor, how nice to see you," Greg, George's son, said, suddenly appearing and taking her hand in both of his. George scowled at him and turned away.

"I'll see what the chef is up to," Greg said as he left.

There was a substantial fire far enough from the tree for safety and Aggie stood before it as she warmed her hands.

"Everything looks so festive," she commented. Of course, she had noticed that the lobby was empty of guests—quite a difference from past visits in the summer when it was bursting with activity. But she decided she liked this quieter version and wondered if they had the place to themselves. Aside from Hextilda and Caroline.

The porter was busy bringing in the Taylors' bags when George saw Rob's car pull up and went to intercept those visitors before they had a chance to unload the car themselves.

John came in with the skis on his shoulder and went to the front desk but saw that nobody was stationed there just a desk bell which he was reluctant to use. "I'm wondering if they have enough staff to support the winter sports enthusiasts," he said, looking very much like one in his thick wool sweater and pants although he still had on his usual fedora.

"Maybe we're some of the few guests," Aggie said.

Finally, George scurried from the front door to the reception desk and checked in the three couples, giving them keys. The men helped the porter carry the luggage into the elevator, deciding to leave the ski equipment on the first floor to be stored in a locked room rather than carrying it up and down each day. Their three rooms were in a row and Louisa made a resigned sigh as Amanda opened the door to theirs.

"Don't start," Amanda said to her sister. "If I were to let you share a room with Rob, I would never hear the end of it from Mother and Daddy."

"Who appointed you to the morality police?" Louisa muttered.

"It's a position that somehow you have put me into. Once Brendan and I are married and I'm out of the house, you'll have to look after yourself."

Louisa put her suitcase onto the stand at the bottom of one of the twin beds. "Never fear. I'll get over it."

"Please do so with some grace."

"I don't suppose we could work a deal with Rob and Brendan…"

"No. Neither of us wants to get into a shotgun wedding situation."

"You sound so puritanical."

"No, practical. Anytime someone has a hurried wedding or a seven-month baby, tongues wag. And they never stop. I'm sure you can remember the looks that certain women get. It's a smear that never goes away. I don't intend to be one of them."

They busied themselves unpacking, glad that the sporty nature of their holiday didn't require fancy dress even for the evenings.

"I'll just freshen up and then go downstairs to take the lay of the land," Amanda said. She washed her face, brushed her chin-length, brown bob into place, put on lipstick and left the room, only to put her head back around the corner a moment later. "We'd better get two keys," she said, Although I can see you can lock the door from the inside with that hand switch," she added and closed the door. Louisa plopped herself on the bed and sighed.

By the time Amanda got downstairs there was a young woman in a service uniform who asked if she might like something to drink.

"Hot cocoa?" Amanda asked and the woman nodded. Aggie and John had just come down and put in an order with the woman as well and they moved in front of the fire.

"How is your room?" Amanda asked.

"Very nice. And thank you so much for the treat. I just hope we'll have these days to ourselves so we can be outside and not interrupted by some crisis medical situation," Aggie said.

"There's bound to be something," John said.

"Don't be resigned to it and, in fact, don't even think it or it will come true," Aggie scolded.

"I'm surprised at what a large place this is," Amanda commented.

"It's often full in the summer. They have tennis and there's a nearby lake for swimming, boating and canoeing. Nothing fancy, but the temperatures are perfect and the views of the mountains gorgeous."

Brendan appeared, rubbing his hands together as he approached the fire. "What's on the agenda?" he asked.

They looked at one another. "Let's wait for the others to come down and we'll make a plan," Aggie suggested. "That poor porter seems to be working all by himself. I can't imagine he's got everyone's stuff delivered."

"Quite an interesting fellow," John said. "From Latin America."

"How do you know that?" Brendan asked.

"I haven't narrowed down his accent yet, but that will be my little game before we're done here. I told him so myself."

"You speak Spanish?" Amanda asked.

"Yes. Spent a few summers in Yucatan working on an archaeological dig during high school. Great fun. Of course, my Spanish is rusty, but I was able to keep up a good conversation. I'm guessing he's from Mexico, but we'll see."

They listened to the crackling of the fire, enjoying the warmth and fellowship until interrupted by a whooping shriek that had them on their feet, thinking there had been some accident. It wasn't a sign of distress, however, it was just Hextilda Browne, who had discovered their presence and was bearing down on them with arms outstretched, her hair partly escaping from a loose bun at the back of her head, and a shawl floating out behind her.

"I can't believe you're here!" she said to Amanda, pulling her into an embrace, then turning to Aggie before remembering their last encounter and greeting her and John more formally. "And who's this handsome young man?" Hextilda asked, sidling up to Brendan, although she had met him before in a different situation.

"Brendan Halloran," he said, holding out his hand to shake hers.

"My fiancé," Amanda added.

"Well, you've done well for yourself, I see."

To Amanda's amusement, Brendan blushed.

"Let's sit down," Hextilda said, pushing her way to the center of the seating on the sofa to be directly in front of the fire. "I don't know why Caroline, who complains bitterly about how cold our house is in Boston, wants to come out here and be cold in a less comfortable setting. Oh, well."

"Will she be down soon?" Amanda asked.

"I expect so."

The server came in and, as she approached the group, Hextilda stood up and took one of the mugs from the tray.

"Hot cocoa. Just the thing." She sat down again, and the server looked perplexed as to what to do since the older woman hadn't been the one who ordered it.

John took the two remaining mugs, handed them to Aggie and Amanda and asked for two more for Brendan and himself.

"Won't this be a lovely time?" Hextilda asked.

Chapter 4

Once the cocoa was consumed, Aggie suggested she and John could keep Hextilda company to allow Amanda and Brendan, now joined by Rob and Louisa, to explore the hotel where they had never been before.

"Thank you," Amanda said with sincerity, always impressed with Aggie's kindness and eager to be out of Fred's mother's presence.

They walked across the broad expanse of the nearly empty lobby to a set of doors.

"Let's see what's in here," Rob said.

Opening the doors, they faced a cavernous, darkened ballroom, but the light from the open door gave them some idea of the size of the place. Brendan whistled at the expanse. The round tables were bare, and chairs were either turned upside down on them or stacked against the wall.

"Look, a bandstand. This must be a hopping place in the summertime."

"Aggie told me when Cash Ridley owned the place, he had out-of-town bands and singers performing. There hadn't been anything like that before."

The kitchens must have been adjacent to the dining room because they could hear the clatter of pans and then raised voices.

"That sounds like the owner again."

They couldn't hear the exact words but there were more than two people engaged in an argument and the banging of metal pans.

Then they heard quite clearly, "Don't forget who the boss is here" and the sound of a swinging door banging open against a wall.

The two couples looked at each other and tiptoed out, closing the doors behind them.

"Rob, do you have to deal with behind-the-scenes outbursts like that at the Oasis?" Amanda asked.

"We're lucky. Our crew has been working together long enough to know what to expect from one another. They started when I started and are as grateful for the success as I am."

"I think it's the tone you set," Louisa said. "You're very calm, no matter what occurs. If the owner shouts and screams, then the staff feel they can do it, too."

"The only problems we've had were from some of the entertainers, and that's why their dressing rooms are at the opposite end of the dining room," Rob said.

"You don't want anyone spoiling the broth," Louisa said.

"I think it's 'too many cooks' spoil the broth," Rob corrected. "In any case, it's a good idea to keep rival musicians and temperamental singers in their own area to sort things out."

From the opposite end of the lobby, they followed a hall that led off to a series of rooms suitable for private parties. They investigated each room, and it occurred to them that they could take their meals in there as a group if they wanted. Continuing down the hallway they found a library.

"We can hide out here," Amanda stage-whispered to Brendan, admiring the deep armchairs scattered in the room. The collection of books suggested it consisted of whatever someone had left behind or forgotten after a visit, as well as guidebooks of the Berkshires and outdated magazines. A map of the Mountain Aire property hung nearby on one wall and opposite it was what appeared to be a diagram of the ski area.

Brendan examined the ski map. "Can that really be the elevation at the top?" he asked.

"I suppose," Amanda said. "I never asked."

"What do the different colors mean?" he asked, tracing them with his finger on the glass of the frame.

"Black for most difficult, blue for intermediate and green for beginners," she said.

"You can also do backcountry skiing," Rob said.

"What does that mean?"

"Skiing outside the marked boundaries of the marked runs. Off-piste, it's called."

"Why would you want to do that?" Brendan asked, furrowing his dark brows.

"It's more of a challenge. You're not skiing in everyone else's ruts. Quite a lot of fun for the adventurous."

"I think I'd better conquer the green one first," Brendan said.

"Good thinking. Did I mention, when I called the lodge, I found that there is an instructor on duty who would be glad to teach you the ropes?" Rob asked.

"I just hope I won't be stuck in a group with a bunch of eight-year-olds who will make me seem totally uncoordinated."

"Not to worry. The locals, even the little ones, are adept at the sport. I bet you'll be the only pupil. I'm sure he'll go easy on you," Amanda said.

Louisa stood at the table in the middle of the room leafing through the **Berkshire Eagle**. "This is several days old. I guess if there aren't many guests, why bother having a current newspaper? I'd be surprised if many visitors would be interested in the engagement party of a local girl or who still has hay for sale."

After examining the photos on the walls of people playing tennis, sailing, hiking, swimming and playing croquet, they pulled books off the shelves, admiring the assortment.

"Let's see what's out back," Brendan said, and they moved into the hallway and out to a wide indoor space that mirrored an outdoor space of the same size. Rob walked over to the floor-to-ceiling windows and surveyed the view.

"Not only do you have the mountains in the background, but you can also probably see any tennis match in progress, at least from the outside." He opened a glass door and let in a blast of cold air before closing it behind him. He trod through the several inches of snow past stacked tables and chairs covered in canvas to the low wall and peered over.

"He'll catch his death," Louisa said, shivering.

Rob only stayed a few moments before quickly retracing his steps and stomping the snow off his shoes onto the carpet, looking sheepish at the mess he made.

"It must be grand in the summer when you can sit outside with a gin and tonic and watch the players. Over to the right the veranda extends around the side of the building." He gestured with his arm. "I bet you can dine out there. Whose idea was it to come in the middle of December, anyway?" he joked.

"At least there are no crowds," Amanda said in her defense. "And the room rates were very reasonable."

"Of course. The only guests are the abominable snowmen," Louisa said.

Brendan laughed. "That's somewhere in the Himalayas, not here. And they call them yetis there. But I have heard of something called Bigfoot lurking in the woods in the Northwest," he said in an ominous tone. "I'll have to ask John if there was anything like that where he grew up."

No sooner were the words out of his mouth than they heard the elevator doors open and a thump in the hall, a pause, and then another thump, as if enormous, heavy feet were making their way laboriously from the elevator to the lobby.

"What's that?" Louisa asked, clutching Rob's arm.

"It's not Bigfoot. I don't think he would know how to operate an elevator. But maybe he was upstairs ransacking the rooms."

"Stop it!" she said. "Let's look and see."

They went back to the hallway and looked around the corner to see the back of a man with a cast on his right leg and crutches slowly navigating his way toward the lobby.

"Phew," Brendan said, comically wiping his brow. "It's human. But wait a minute. Why does he have a cast? I thought you said skiing was perfectly safe," he said to Amanda.

She shrugged and smiled. They had to wait for dinner to find out the source of the injury of the mystery man, and he didn't need to tell them as Hextilda was more than happy to supply the information. She ambushed them as they were making their way to the dining room, pulled Amanda aside and whispered a short version of what would be a longer version later.

"Not a ski accident," she reassured her. "He slipped somewhere on the ice in Pittsfield, got his leg set and decided to stay here for a bit before going back home. Poor Sergei. I think he would have been better off in Pittsfield with a better choice of hotels," she said, looking over her shoulder to see if the Fosters or their staff might have overheard. "This is rather primitive, don't you think? They don't have many people working here, so I don't even know if they have the capacity for room service."

If so, why was she here, Amanda thought.

The man in question was seated at a far table set for two with his crutches propped against the wall. He winced as he adjusted himself in the chair, trying to find an appropriate place to set his leg.

"He certainly gets around quite ably," Brendan said, wondering if he were to be the one who landed in a cast in the next few days whether he would fare as well.

"I'm sorry to desert you young folks, but I'm going to keep the dear man company." Hextilda waved her hand at him and moved off in a swirl of scarves and perfume.

"That's funny, I don't remember inviting her to our table in the first place," Louisa said.

The Taylors were already seated and motioned the others forward. John stood to pull a chair out for Amanda.

"Tell me, is the food here good?" Amanda asked her cousin.

"I've always thought so. I don't know if they have the same chef that Cash Ridley employed, but as long as they've kept his recipes, we'll be all right. Maybe they even have fresh game. Wouldn't that be great?"

A waitress came up to their table to hand menus around and stopped short when she saw John.

"Hello," he said politely and recognized her as the young woman who had come to his office the day before, although he didn't want to embarrass her. She almost hid her hands behind her back, thinking everyone would notice the red and swollen fingers. The others had seen her so briefly in John's office that they didn't notice the woman's discomfort.

"Is there anything you can recommend?" Amanda asked her.

"The duck à l'orange is a specialty of the chef," she said. "But the prime rib is excellent, too. Would you like something to drink first?"

"Cocktails or wine?" Rob asked, and the group decided martinis all around were a good idea. She hesitated as if waiting for another question and then went back to the kitchen.

"Wasn't that?" Aggie said, following the woman with her eyes before looking back again. John continued to look at the menu. "I recognized her hands," she added.

"You don't miss much, do you?" her husband said with a smile.

"She's quite thin. You would think that anyone working in a place that serves food would have a little more meat on her bones," Aggie said.

"Maybe that's how the owners cut corners," Rob said.

"Our room is perfectly comfortable with the radiators functioning, but maybe they have the staff sleep in cold attic rooms, hence the chilblains," Amanda observed.

"It must cost a fortune to heat this place," Louisa said. She looked up and saw Caroline stride into the dining room, stop and come over to their table.

"Greetings, strangers."

Rob, Brendan and John stood up. "I don't believe you know our cousin Aggie and her husband, John," Amanda said as Caroline shook hands with them both.

"How is your vacation so far?" Louisa asked her.

"Ghastly," she whispered. "But the skiing is wonderful. I practically had the runs to myself today. I say, I've got a strange thing to ask of you." She twisted her hands together, trying to look coy. "Would you mind awfully if I dined with you? My mother and I see enough of each other as it is, and she is totally absorbed in that gentleman with the cast." She turned and waved vaguely in their direction with a smile.

"Not at all," Rob said, and took a chair from an adjacent table and brought it over, positioning it between himself and Louisa, who knew Caroline best. She looked over Louisa's shoulder at the menu and pointed.

"The roast chicken was excellent last night, but I'll try something else tonight." She fished in her purse and pulled out a small case. "Do you mind if I smoke?" she asked. They might not have been smokers themselves but politely said it was not a problem.

"We've just ordered martinis all around," Rob said. "Would you like one?"

"Oh, yes," she said.

Rob got up and headed toward the kitchen to intercept the waitress.

"Oh, I didn't mean to be so much trouble," Caroline said.

"What a coincidence that we are all here," Louisa said. "What is your mother doing if she isn't skiing?"

Caroline sighed. "This isn't just a holiday, actually. It is truly a getaway. My mother told me she received a threat of me being kidnapped in Boston and both José and my mother thought it best that we make ourselves scarce."

The group was momentarily shocked into silence.

"Why didn't you call the police?" Brendan asked. "That's serious business."

Caroline hesitated. "José thinks it has something to do with his family's enemies back home. We could scarcely call out the American authorities to assist with a foreign threat."

"You absolutely could. And should." Brendan said. "What is it you're not telling us?"

Caroline looked down and took a drag of her cigarette while she pondered how to answer.

Rob came back and looked perplexed by the changed atmosphere at the table.

"What's going on?" he asked.

"Caroline was just going to reveal why a kidnap threat against her shouldn't be a matter for the police," Louisa said in exasperation.

"Well, you know that José's family had to leave their homeland," Caroline said to Rob and Louisa. "They'd lived there for generations. The Guzmáns were wealthy and prominent and when they sensed a political change was about to happen, they transferred what funds they could to the States. It seems every fifty years or so that sort of thing happens. I suppose they didn't support the right people. Or bribe them enough. His father put their plantations in the care of the bishop with the understanding that if they should return, the ownership would revert to the Guzmán family."

"How do they know that the bishop will make good on his promise?" Amanda asked.

"The family has supported the church financially for generations. But there is something else that affords them protection. I don't know what and they wouldn't tell me. Those now in power don't dare touch the clergy or what they do, so José's family think they are in a safe position. Until the next coup d'état."

"Why have they targeted you?" Brendan asked.

"I don't know. Easy target? In their home country, wealthy women are housebound, raising a family and dealing with the household. Women there never go out alone and, if they do go out, it's often with a male relative or a guard."

"How do they get anything done?" Aggie asked.

"Everything comes to them. Food, clothing, everything is delivered. Hairdressers, manicurists, dressmakers and shoe salespeople all make house calls. The women never have to leave the house. That's why their homes are actually compounds enclosed in walls that border the street with gardens inside. Sort of like a castle with a moat. Quite the opposite of how we build our houses and live. I'm more visible because I am out and about, often by myself. Once this blows over, I'll probably have to have an armed companion."

That silenced the others at the table as they thought of the implications. The waitress interrupted the mood as she wheeled in a trolley with glasses and a pitcher of martinis. She poured them out carefully and, when she was done, asked if there were any questions about the menu and if they were ready to order. Despite their fascination with Caroline's tale, they had each made up their minds and responded. After the waitress left, they held up their glasses in a toast to their company and took a first sip.

"Oh, I certainly needed that," Caroline said.

"Changing the subject, how is the skiing? I hope it's not too icy," Amanda said.

"Well, it's not the pure powder you get out West, but it snowed since the last weekend's usual traffic, so I think you'll enjoy it. After a full day out there, I'll be ready to turn in shortly after dinner. Not that there's any nightlife to speak of."

A middle-aged couple stood by the doorway to the dining room, hesitating as if waiting for a maître d' to escort them in. Looking around and finally realizing that things were less formal than they had expected, they made their way to a nearby table, nodding to the large group as they went.

"Academics," Caroline pronounced.

"Do you know them?" Aggie asked.

"No. The name is Dalrymple. I'm just surmising from the tweed jacket and suede elbow patches that he teaches some stuffy subject in a small college. I wouldn't be surprised if he pulls out a pipe after dinner. They just got here today, too. He actually was wearing a deerstalker hat earlier."

"Now you've got me intrigued," Amanda said. "I'll have to do a little investigating at tomorrow's buffet-style breakfast. Start up a casual conversation and all."

"She's a licensed private investigator now, you know," Brendan said to Caroline.

"I didn't know. What luck! Maybe you can help me unravel this supposed kidnap plot," Caroline said, looking at her.

Amanda had an urge to kick Brendan under the table but merely said, "I'd better leave that to more experienced and professional hands," looking at her fiancé with a tight smile.

Their attention was drawn to a yelp from Hextilda's table when the porter—now in his role as a waiter—approached. Her hand flew to her chest, clutching her necklace with a look of fear. The man excused himself and backed away and a female waitress took his place.

Caroline rolled her eyes. "He's the one with the Spanish accent so, of course, she assumes he's going to whisk me away. He's hardly the size to intimidate anyone. Even if I were spirited away, it's not likely that Fred or my mother would pay to rescue me!" She laughed at her joke.

"It's a good thing you have José. You know he is absolutely devoted to you," Rob said with a serious face.

"Yes, I know it. I'm a lucky girl."

She might have thought so, but one look between Amanda and Louisa confirmed that they would rather be in any other family than the Brownes.

Chapter 5

The three couples and Caroline enjoyed a leisurely dinner, accompanied by a bottle of wine and animated conversation, outlasting the Professor, as he had been dubbed, and his wife.

The man with the cast on his leg had excused himself from Hextilda's company and struggled to pull himself to his feet. Rather than sporting long pants, he wore plus fours to accommodate the cast on his one leg while the other was covered with an argyle sock and a normal shoe making for a bizarre appearance. He managed to get his crutches in place and slowly made his way out of the dining room, nodding to the large table but not stopping to talk.

Moments later, Hextilda floated their way and asked no one in particular to fetch her a chair so she could join them. She promptly sat down when one was pulled from an adjacent table, plopping her large handbag on the tabletop with a thump.

"Mother?" Caroline asked, looking down at the handbag.

Ignoring her daughter completely, she said rather than asked, "Isn't the food surprisingly good? I mean for a place out in the country." Her eyes followed the man with the cast until he was out of the room. "Oh, the poor man!"

"That's got to be very exhausting to get around on crutches all the time," Amanda said.

"He probably ought to have a wheelchair, but if he's by himself, there's no one to push it," Aggie said. "Sometimes it's better to have that exercise during the recuperation, however. If he were lying about in bed all day, his muscles would atrophy and that would be another thing to contend with."

"He doesn't complain about it at all. His mind is on other, more important things," Hextilda said, brushing a lock of hair that had escaped from the improvised loose bun at the back of her head. Not getting a word of inquiry from the others about what she was referring to, she continued. "I'm thinking of asking him to stay with us when we go home."

"Oh, Mother, really!" Caroline said. "We're already packed to the rafters at home with Valerie moving in after the wedding." Amanda and Brendan exchanged a look.

"It will make for a jolly six at the dinner table."

Caroline rolled her eyes.

"There's the guest bedroom, you know," Hextilda said.

"You simply can't. It's the overflow space for my gowns. And our out-of-season clothes are in the closet there. You don't imagine we'll store all that in the attic. Traipsing up and down the stairs to that freezing space every time I need a change of clothes. It's cruel."

"He could always camp out in the library," her mother replied.

"Why can't Fred and Valerie get their own place? He certainly makes enough as a physician. And you couldn't put that man in the library. Fred would never stand for it. And neither would I. There's little privacy as it is. Where would we go for peace and quiet to read? Why must you bring every sorry soul under our roof?"

"You can't imagine the strain Sergei has been under. Trying to raise money and the price keeps getting higher."

"Is that his name?"

"Yes, Sergei Rostov."

"Like the family in War and Peace?" Brendan asked.

"What are you talking about?" Caroline asked, ignoring the comment about his name.

"There are certain people still in hiding in Russia who need to be rescued, but it takes money to do that," Hextilda said.

"Who, for instance? His family?" Caroline asked.

"I can't say. But it's costly to get a forged passport, the proper clothes and a reliable network to make it happen." She clamped her mouth shut as the others looked wide-eyed at her.

"Is he smuggling people out?" Caroline asked, looking horrified at the notion.

"If only he were so lucky to succeed. But I will assist him in any way I can."

"I hope you're not thinking of giving him money for this vague rescue mission for unnamed people," Caroline said. "If he's caught, I'm sure the Russians will execute him."

Her mother was silent.

"Honestly, that's the limit. We scrimp and save and you're giving money to a complete stranger for another nameless complete stranger?"

"I said nothing of the kind. I think I'll tuck in for the night," Hextilda said, getting up and without further words, sailing out of the room.

"Is there any more wine in that bottle?" Caroline asked.

"Just a tad," Rob said, pouring half a glass for her.

"Maybe we need a refill on the martinis," Amanda whispered to Brendan.

"Who is this man, anyway?" Caroline asked. "I think I need to talk to my brother. My mother has been eccentric, as everyone has noted, but I think she's gone gaga. We may have to do something with her." She drank the rest of the wine quickly.

"Don't jump to conclusions," John advised. "Of course, I don't know your mother." He looked over at Aggie because she knew that he had been exposed to enough of the woman's behavior to make an assessment but now declined. "She just may be agitated by world events and perhaps the simple solution is not to leave her alone with this Svengali."

"That's a good idea," Amanda said. "It might be uncomfortable, but we need to wean her from this man's influence or fantasies."

"Are you willing to babysit?" Caroline asked. "We could take turns. Maybe that nice couple who had dinner here tonight could befriend her. She's not participating in winter sports and they don't look like the outdoorsy type. How's this: I'll take the breakfast duty and then someone can stay with her until lunch."

"I suppose I could do that," Aggie said.

"Wonderful. We'll all have lunch here rather than at the resort. Better yet, why don't we have one of the staff look after her? The waitress? The porter?" Amanda asked, trying to come to Aggie's rescue.

Caroline laughed. "Are you mad? She probably suspects that the porter is the mastermind behind the alleged kidnapping scheme." She got up. "Let me give this some thought. My mother is more dangerous than you may think. Didn't you notice how heavy her handbag was? It's because she's brought a gun with her on our holiday to protect us. God help us that she doesn't use it."

The remaining party was agog and silent as Caroline left the dining room, then broke into overlapping declarations of regret for having offered assistance the next day.

"What was I thinking?" Aggie said, holding her head in her hands.

"You've got to stop being the good Girl Scout," Amanda answered.

"This calls for some drastic action. We'll just make ourselves unavailable in the morning," John suggested.

"That will just thrust the responsibility on Amanda or Louisa," Aggie said.

"Why is it that the womenfolk are the only ones being considered for the caretaking role?" Louisa asked. "Don't they always refer to men in white coats taking people away? Maybe one of the staff could babysit her. If worse comes to worse, I'm sure there is some handy-dandy sedative in the little black bag you carry, John."

"Really!" Amanda said to her sister. "I think we've had enough excitement for tonight. Let's go to bed," she said, getting up and pulling her sister to a standing position. "Good night, all. I'm sure it will sort itself out in the morning."

Chapter 6

Things sorted themselves out when Caroline met them at the buffet breakfast and announced that her mother wasn't feeling well and would stay in her room at least until lunchtime.

"I'm sorry to hear that," Aggie said, mustering a sincere face. However, she declined to offer John's services as doctor in the house; that would require a request from the patient, and she was reluctant to spoil her husband's rare holiday.

The buffet was a hearty offering of pancakes, eggs, sausage, bacon, toast and oatmeal laid out on a sideboard for guests to serve themselves.

"I guess they think we normally eat like lumberjacks," Brendan said. "Or is skiing that physically taxing?"

"I guess you'll find out," Amanda said with a smirk.

"You won't be laughing when they haul me back here with two broken legs."

"That's why we brought John along," she said. "Just in case."

Brendan piled his plate high and walked uncomfortably to a nearby table, hindered by the bulky wool pants and long johns underneath, more layers of clothing than he normally wore. John was already seated, looking in his element, his broad chest encased in a Norwegian sweater and his cheeks rosy from the warmth of the room. Louisa and Amanda were in slim-fitting wool pants and turtleneck sweaters, saving the heavier outer gear to put on just before leaving the hotel.

The middle-aged couple from the previous night stood at the doorway to the dining room, scanning the area for a place to sit and choosing a table near the larger party. Friendly nods were given to them as they passed and Caroline muttered, "I think their name is the Tweeds." Louisa stifled a giggle.

Amanda gave her a look. "Don't laugh. You'll be dressed like that in another twenty years."

"Not on your life. I intend to be swathed in silk and a full-length fur coat," was her reply.

The man hesitated at pulling out a chair for his wife before turning back to Amanda's group and walking over with her. "I'm Alvan Dalrymple. This is my wife, Martha." She joined him, hesitantly blinking behind her wire rim glasses.

Introductions were made and the man said, "Actually, Professor Dalrymple. History is my bailiwick. Say, are you related to Ambrose Burnside?" he asked Amanda.

"No, afraid not."

"Now don't be shy about it." He stroked his short beard carefully. "He was a very capable man who was promoted out of his depth. A very smart man, such a shame, wasn't it?"

Louisa, not one for history asked, "What happened?"

"Surely your parents must have told you the tragedy of Uncle Ambrose." He chuckled and his wife joined in.

"Really, he wasn't a relation," Amanda said.

Not to be stopped, the Professor continued. "A West Point graduate who became a brigadier general. Union Army, lucky for you." He chortled. "Took a lot of heat for not supporting McClellan better at Antietam. And then got appointed commander of the Army of the Potomac. See, you needn't be coy about your connection."

Amanda held her tongue, sure this man wouldn't let go of the mistaken relationship and hoping he would soon get to Appomattox Court House and be done with the Civil War.

"And just when he thought he had victory and honor in his grasp, there was the defeat at Fredericksburg. Oh, poor Uncle Ambrose. Try as he might, it was one debacle after another and, finally, a resignation. But don't worry, after the war he acquitted himself as a governor and senator from your home state of Rhode Island."

"Actually, we're from Boston," Amanda corrected him.

Attempting to save the situation, John asked him "What brings you to this neck of the woods?"

"Not a ski holiday for us," his wife chuckled.

"The semester has ended so we decided to come over from Troy for a few days."

"Are you at the Teachers' College?" John asked.

"No, at the Emma Willard School. We both work there."

"I've heard wonderful things about that place," Amanda said.

The couple smiled. "Please, don't let us interrupt your breakfast. We'll just grab a bite before going out for the day."

"No trouble at all," John said, sitting back down. "They seem like a nice couple."

Amanda and Louisa stared at him.

"The man was a complete bore," Louisa said.

"I wonder where they'll be going today. Kind of a strange time to be sightseeing," Aggie said.

"What do you say? Forty minutes to departure?" John asked Aggie as he finished his meal.

"Or sooner," she replied. "I don't want to get ambushed at the last minute," meaning that she was not too sure that Caroline might not once again prevail upon her to stay with Hextilda. She had already brought her outerwear down to make certain of a fast getaway.

"What runs are you thinking of attempting?" Rob asked John. "You look like a black diamond sort of man."

John laughed. "More like diamond in the rough. I haven't been since last year and I wish I were in better shape for it. Back in the day, I used to gear up for ski season with specific exercises. Now it seems I spend my days sitting too much."

"We're probably all guilty of that," Rob said.

"How did you learn to ski?" Louisa asked her boyfriend.

While he pondered how to answer, Caroline butted in. "Some former girlfriend, no doubt. Probably in Switzerland."

"Something like that," Rob said with a smile. He had grown up with a single mother and tight finances—not a likely candidate to pursue that sport on his own. Nor had he ever been to Europe.

"Such a man of mystery, Louisa. How can you stand it?" Caroline teased, to her friend's discomfort.

"I'm going to start out on the easy slope to test out the quality of the snow before going far up the mountain," Aggie said. "Sometimes it's icy and that's not for me."

"Good plan. I'll go with you," Amanda said. "What's our departure time, Rob?"

"Whenever you're ready."

They hurried to finish their breakfast, not just to get an early start on the day, but to avoid getting drawn into Hextilda's drama or another mistaken genealogy cum history lesson from the Professor.

The waitress who had come out to replenish their coffee—they later learned she was Greg Foster's wife—informed them that this was the staff's half day, and they ought to take their lunch at the ski lodge since the chef and everyone else would be gone into Pittsfield. John and Aggie knew the offerings at the ski lodge were simpler than what they might get at the hotel, but as long as it was warm and filling, they didn't care.

The caravan of two cars took off with Caroline getting a ride with John and Aggie, where there was more room and she felt she could avail herself of his professional advice if she provided him details of her mother's ailments.

"Usually when I'm in a social situation and someone asks me about their health, I tell them to step in the next room, get undressed and we'll see." He laughed.

She did not.

"A doctor joke," he explained.

"Well, if you don't mind, perhaps you could check up on her when we get back. I'm sure it's nothing serious. She's sort of a high-strung person."

"I hadn't noticed," he said with a straight face and Aggie swatted him in the leg out of sight of their passenger in the back seat.

"Oh, yes. She worries about Fred and me, about the house and those pesky characters in her books, too."

Aggie turned around to see if Caroline was joking.

"It's true. They are almost real to her, and she's even said if she doesn't write for a few days, they start their conversations in her head."

"Interesting," John said, raising one eyebrow.

They pulled up to the ski lodge ten minutes later and were pleased to see that there were not too many cars in the parking lot. A plume of smoke arose from the Swiss-style building, promising warm drinks and hot food for the day.

"How about we meet back at the lodge at noon?" John asked Aggie.

"Sounds good." They each carried their skis over their shoulders, poles in hand, and walked in their boots across the lot to the back of the building where they could see other pairs of skis either sticking upright in the snow or leaning against the building.

Brendan had been looking forward to the new experience but apprehensive at having his booted feet tied to the skis with leather straps, snug between the toe and heel iron with nothing to stop his fall but the ski poles. While the others went to the base of the mountain, he went inside and inquired about the appointment he had made with a ski instructor and encountered a sturdy young woman who said she was Hope and asked if he was Brian.

"No, Brendan. First-timer here. Go easy on me. And I may need more than hope."

She laughed in response.

"Are there other students?"

"No, it's a one-on-one. You'll be sailing down the mountain by the end of the day."

"As long as I'm intact, that's what counts."

His fears of being run over by the experts—and that included Amanda—were alleviated when she took him to a quiet part of the slope, strapped him into the skis and showed him the basics of angling the skis inward, what she called the snowplow.

"It will feel slow and awkward at first, but if you ever find yourself going too fast, employ the snowplow. A natural instinct when you attempt to slow down is to sit down. But you'll go faster, be on your rear and not be able to stop."

Then she took away his poles and they practiced concentrating on his lower body control without the distraction of the poles. The time flew by, and he felt more confident by the minute until she told him it was time for a break. He managed to awkwardly ski back to the base of the lodge, unstrap the bindings and go inside for a needed cup of coffee.

"Ten-minute break, and then back to the salt mines," Hope said.

They continued working until noon and she suggested they meet the next morning when he would be going up the rope tow.

Brendan spotted Amanda in the lodge's dining room in her orange hat and red scarf not yet removed after coming inside.

"How did it go?" she asked.

"That's hard work," he said.

"Look, there are the others," Amanda said, spotting the rest of their group and waving them over. "It's cafeteria style with simple selections like hot dogs, hamburgers and hot soup."

They made their way to the line of other skiers and looked around for Caroline.

"I saw her on one run but not since then. She'll catch up to us."

A man came up to them and, looking at the men, asked if anyone was Doctor Taylor. Aggie's face fell, knowing there was something that he needed to attend to.

"Is there a problem with someone here?" John asked.

"No. Telephone call for you."

"No rest for the weary," Aggie said. She stepped away from the line as John followed the man out of the room, waiting to see what he would need to do. A few minutes later, he returned.

"Mrs. Parsons fell and may have broken her hip. They took her to the hospital, but she was adamant that I be there. I'll go back to the hotel and make a quick change before heading out."

"Do you want me to come?" Aggie asked.

"Not necessary."

As he started toward the door, Brendan stopped him. "Do you mind if I grab a ride back to the hotel with you? I think I'm done for the day."

"Are you sure?"

"I know when to stop before I injure myself," he said. "I've already told Amanda."

"Let's get our skis, rather than leaving that task for the others in a crowded car."

"A broken hip is a bad thing, from what I've heard," Brendan said as they tied the skis to the roof of the car.

"It's always bad, especially if you're an older woman. And this particular woman lives by herself and is ferociously independent. I'm sure she put up a fight about going to the hospital in the first place."

They drove in silence to the hotel and John parked the car outside the front door.

"Go ahead and change," Brendan said. "I'll get the equipment inside." It didn't take long to free the bulky wooden skis from the roof, haul them over to the building and lean them against the brick façade. He wondered if he should put them back in the storage area he had retrieved them from and went into the lobby to ask for assistance, but no one was behind the front desk. No one was in the lobby and he didn't want to call out and make a ruckus. Then he remembered that it was the staff's half day, which explained why nobody was there. It was still odd to leave the empty building unlocked.

John came jogging down the corridor after changing his clothes and gave Brendan a pat on the back.

"Don't know when I'll be back. But I'll call later," he said rushing out to the car.

Brendan brought the skis inside, left them leaning against the lobby wall and went in search of either someone or the location of the storage room. He went down the long hall they had walked down the day before when exploring and found the room that the porter had taken the skis from just that morning. He pulled on the handle and found it locked.

"Of course." He wondered if it made more sense to just haul the skis up to the room, but it would be a clumsy trip down the hall with two sets of skis and poles, not to mention leaving a mess with melting snow. Somebody had to be around to let him into the room. He looked into the library and each of the private rooms but saw nobody. Then he approached a perpendicular hallway that seemed to be the service area where food was brought from the kitchen out to the dining room. A round window in a closed swinging door gave a view of the kitchen, where a tall glass of water stood on the metal prep table. Someone had to be in there. He pushed the door open. His eye was immediately struck by a pair of feet sticking out behind the prep table. Brendan rushed around thinking the chef may have fainted and instead saw the porter with a bullet hole in his chest and a blossom of blood on his uniform jacket. He put his hand on the man's neck to check for a pulse as a matter of form, although he knew for certain that the man was already dead.

Chapter 7

Brendan's first instinct was to see if John was still outside, but he knew too much time had passed from when he began his search for the storage room. He looked around quickly to see if anyone was hiding, but all was quiet so he raced to the lobby in the hopes that someone might have appeared behind the front desk in his absence.

All was quiet.

He went behind the front desk and opened a drawer searching for a telephone book and found a thin one with numbers for the county only. In the business section, he found the Greylock Ski Lodge and dialed the number. It hadn't been that long since he and John had left the others, and they were likely still in the cafeteria. After explaining it was an emergency to the woman who answered the phone, she offered to call the Sheriff. He declined, intending to do that himself after relaying the message that everyone of their party should come back immediately. Next, he found the number for the Sheriff and calling, explained that someone had died under suspicious circumstances.

No sooner had he hung up the phone than the Fosters, father, son and his wife, their arms laden with packages, came through the front doors into the lobby. They stopped in surprise at seeing him behind the desk but said nothing.

"I'm afraid your employee, Tony, is dead."

"What?"

"He's in the kitchen."

They dropped the packages and rushed down the hall with Brendan calling out behind them, "Don't touch anything. The Sheriff is on the way."

They had already pushed their way through the swinging door and stood transfixed at the foot of the porter's body.

"He's been shot," Greg said, pointing to the red blood stain on the chest of his white uniform. His wife gasped from the doorway where she stood frozen.

George rested his hand on the prep table and leaned over for a closer look, knocking the glass of water over. Out of habit, he grabbed a nearby towel and mopped it up.

"Please don't touch anything else. I don't have any jurisdiction here, but I'm a police officer from Boston and the protocol is to touch nothing. There may be fingerprints or other clues that they'll want to see."

"Look, there's a gun!" George said pointing under the adjacent storage area for pots and pans. He started in that direction, but Brendan put a hand on his arm, and then George realized his mistake and hesitated.

"We'd better go out and wait for the Sheriff."

"I'll stay here," the son said, and Brendan shook his head. "Let's all go out to the lobby."

They stood in the lobby looking out the windows for the approach of a car until George claimed he needed to sit down. Looking over at him, Brendan could see his face had lost color and he was sure the older man was close to passing out.

"Put your head between your knees," Brendan said and told the man to breathe slowly and deeply. It was a full ten minutes before he put his head back upright and slouched into the back of the couch.

"Better, Dad?" the son asked.

"What a shock," was the answer.

They were silent and all joined him on the couch, waiting another ten minutes before they heard a car pull up outside and brisk footsteps enter the lobby. A tall, burly man looked around swiftly and saw two men who had jumped to their feet, a woman seated nearby and the owner next to her.

"What's going on here, George?"

He looked at Brendan, who spoke up. "I'm Brendan Halloran, a guest here. I discovered a body in the kitchen. The man has been shot and he's dead."

"Show me," he said and let Brendan lead the way down one hall and then off to another to the entrance to the kitchen.

Brendan and Greg stood near the foot of the porter's body and the Sheriff pushed his hat back on his head and put his hands on his hips. "Who's this?"

"Tony Rivers. He was working here as a porter and waiter as needed," Greg said.

"Anybody touch anything?"

"No," they answered in unison.

The man looked at Brendan. "What were you doing in the kitchen? Was anybody else in here?"

"No, I came back early from skiing and was looking for someone to help me lock up the skis. But there was nobody in the lobby or any of the downstairs rooms. I ended up looking in here and discovered him. By the way, I'm a detective sergeant with the Boston Police on vacation here."

"Oh, you are, are you." He looked Brendan up and down.

"This is Sheriff Daniels," Greg said.

After a moment, the Sheriff put his big hand out to shake Brendan's. "I probably could use some assistance. One of the deputies has the grippe and the other one is holding down the fort."

"There's a gun, too," Greg said, pointing to it.

"That yours?" he asked the young man.

"No. I've got hunting rifles, but I don't own a handgun."

But Brendan remembered who in the hotel did.

The Sheriff took a clean towel from the top of a pile stacked nearby and carefully lifted the gun into it.

They heard a commotion coming from the direction of the lobby with women and men calling out for Brendan. He ran out and down the hallway. "I'm down here."

Amanda rushed up to him. "Are you all right? What's happened?"

"The porter has been shot. I didn't want to leave that message when I called the ski lodge—I didn't want to alarm everyone."

"Well, I'm alarmed now! Were you here when it happened?"

"No, it must have occurred just before I got back to the hotel."

"Is John still here?" Aggie asked, catching up to them. "He could help."

"John took off for Pittsfield to attend to his patient. And he can't help anyway. The man is dead."

Amanda put her hand to her mouth. "How horrible!"

Brendan turned to go back to the kitchen as Rob and Louisa entered the lobby.

"What's going on?" she asked her sister and was told all that was known.

"Where's Caroline? Did you leave her at the lodge?"

"We couldn't find her," Rob said. "I could go back and look for her."

They stood around the fireplace while Rob placed wood on the embers and, using a bellows, made the fire come back to life.

"Maybe I should call the hospital in Pittsfield and get John back out here if his patient is stabilized. He might be able to determine the cause of death. I mean the timing of the death," Aggie said.

"Murder, you mean," Amanda added.

They looked at one another in trepidation that such a thing could happen in this setting.

"What on earth is going on?" Caroline asked as she walked carefully from the elevator dressed in casual clothes, not her ski attire, and limping a bit.

"Where have you been?" Amanda asked.

"I twisted my knee, so I hitched a ride back with someone who was leaving the lodge. He was kind enough to make a detour and let me off at the front door."

No one said anything.

"I've seen cars coming and going. What's happened?"

"The porter is dead," Aggie said, watching Caroline's face closely.

"What? How? Some accident?"

"Nobody's sure, but the Sheriff is here, and he'll want to talk to all of us. How long have you been back?"

"An hour and a half or so. The lobby was deserted and, since I was hobbling already, I left my skis just inside the door. It was a good thing I had come back since my mother was hysterical."

"About what?" Amanda asked.

"Not sure. I think she's got a fever and that can discombobulate her mind at times. I gave her a half dose of sleeping powder and dozed off myself."

The three Burnside women looked at each other, telegraphing without words that Hextilda's state of mind was likely not due to a fever. And why her daughter put her to sleep was a strange treatment for whatever was wrong with her. Perhaps that was routine for the volatile woman.

Sheriff Daniels came down the hall, his large body as imposing as his scowl as he confronted the group in front of the fire. Without asking, they introduced themselves and then Aggie asked if she should call Doctor Taylor back to examine the body since they were all staying at the hotel anyway.

"Someone in Pittsfield will do the autopsy, but yes, if your husband could come back and estimate time of death, that would be helpful."

"He was alive at nine this morning," Caroline offered.

The Sheriff looked hard at her. "How do you know?"

"Right after breakfast, I saw him in the hallway unloading boxes into the kitchen and someone yelling at him."

"Who might that have been?"

Sorry that she had offered that piece of information, Caroline stammered, "I, I don't know. A man's voice." She looked at the group for support and then sheepishly at the Fosters, who were standing nearby. "Didn't any of you hear it?"

No one responded.

"Well, I can't imagine it was one of our party. We didn't know the man. Perhaps it was one of the Fosters." She looked around again for support, but only received glares in return.

The Sheriff saw George and Greg Foster and asked them how many guests were in the hotel.

"Just this group, a single man and a couple. The couple left for a day trip of some kind and the man, a Mr. Rostov, is laid up with a broken leg. Oh, and Mrs. Browne, this lady's mother," he said gesturing to Caroline, "was in her room."

"How many staff do you have here?"

"We're at bare bones in the winter, as you know. Greg and myself, Jimmy the chef, my daughter-in-law, Eunice," he nodded in her direction, "and Olive. The women do the rooms and serve the food. And the porter."

"Where are Olive and Jimmy?"

"Half-day off."

"Are they upstairs?"

"No, they both went into town. We dropped them off after breakfast. When they call, we'll pick them up."

"The porter didn't go?"

"He said he wanted to stay here."

The Sheriff paused and looked at Caroline. "I think I need to talk to your mother."

Chapter 8

"I'm not sure she's up to it," Caroline said as they got out of the elevator.

The Sheriff didn't respond. He followed Caroline, who opened the unlocked door.

"Mother?" she called out.

A pitiful voice emerged from the bundled covers on one bed.

"Is that you?"

"Yes. There's been an incident, and the Sheriff would like to talk to you."

"I couldn't possibly. I don't feel well."

Caroline spread her hands out in surrender as she looked at the Sheriff.

"I'm afraid we have to talk, no matter how you feel," Daniels said, moving closer to the bed. The tousled gray hair slowly appeared and then the frightened eyes of the woman came into view.

"That's better," he said in a friendly tone.

"Now, do you always leave your room unlocked?" he asked.

Caroline explained, "I was just going downstairs to see what was going on. We weren't thinking when we checked in and only got one key. I took it with me today when we went to the lodge. I figured Mother wouldn't need it."

"And you left the door unlocked?" he asked.

"She can lock it from the inside with the knob." After a moment she added, "I only unlocked when I came back earlier."

"When was that?"

She looked at her wristwatch. "About an hour and a half ago."

The Sheriff looked from one woman to the other and then addressed Hextilda. "Did you leave your room at any time?"

She paused for a long moment. "Yes, I was feeling a bit hungry and thought I'd pop downstairs and get some tea or toast."

"And?"

"It was very quiet. I went to the dining room, thinking that perhaps they were still cleaning up, but it was empty." She clutched the blankets beneath her chin. "Then I followed my nose and saw the light shining out of the porthole window into the hallway. And I approached." She paused for a long moment. "I pushed the door open and saw a man lying on the floor. Well, his feet, that is. I peeked around the table in the middle of the room and saw he was probably dead."

"Mother!"

"Probably?" the Sheriff asked.

"I was too frightened to check, but I'm sure he was. So, I ran back upstairs," she said in a rush of words.

"You ran up the stairs?" the Sheriff asked.

"No, I went to the elevator. My hand was shaking so hard, I almost couldn't push the button. When I got up to the floor, I ran to our room, dashed in and locked the door."

"Mother, why didn't you tell me this?" Caroline said.

"I...I don't know! I'm sure he was the man come to kidnap Caroline and maybe one of his gang was nearby and they had an argument about the ransom or something."

"Kidnap! What gang? What ransom?"

Caroline collapsed into the armchair next to the bed and put her head in her hands.

Sheriff Daniels pulled a straight chair from the desk and turned it to face the frightened woman in the bed. "Start at the very beginning, please."

"My son-in-law received a note suggesting a kidnap of my daughter was going to take place. That's why we're here. Hiding out, as it were. Everything seemed fine and then I spotted the man carrying in our bags. A man with an accent and I do know my accents, sir. His native tongue was likely Spanish, and it just so happens that my son-in-law hails from a Spanish-speaking country. One that he and his family had fled due to political unrest and violence. They can't go back until there is a change in regime and those monsters at the helm would like nothing better than to kill off the entire Guzmán family!"

The Sheriff's eyebrows were nearly up in his hairline as she finished her recital.

"Did they demand a ransom?"

"No, not yet. But that would have been the next stage in the process."

"Back to your visit to the kitchen. About what time was this that you went downstairs?"

"Sometime after everyone left to go ski. I didn't look at the clock."

Turning to Caroline, he said, "And you've been back—it would now be about an hour and a half?"

"That's right."

"Did you happen to go into the kitchen?"

"Me? Of course not. Why would I?"

"To get your mother a bite to eat?" the Sheriff suggested.

"She was agitated when I got back." She looked over to her mother. "So I gave her something so she would sleep."

"How did you spend your time when you got back?"

"I changed my clothes, as you can guess," she said indicating the casual clothing she wore rather than a ski outfit. "Well, I took a bath first, before I changed. And then I read a book I brought with me and drifted off to sleep myself."

"You never returned to the lobby or left the room.?"

"No. Only when I heard the approach of cars and was curious as to what was going on. That's when I went downstairs."

"Were you afraid of the porter?" Daniels asked.

"No. He was a small, sturdy person and, frankly, I didn't buy into my mother's theory of who he was. He acted like a porter and a waiter. Which is what I thought he was."

"Isn't there some other gentleman staying here?" Daniels asked.

"Yes, he and my mother struck up an acquaintance. But I don't know what room he is in."

The Sheriff thanked the two women and went back to the lobby, shaking his head at the strange notions of the mother and the complete disregard of danger on the part of the daughter.

"George, may I speak with you privately?"

The owner brought the Sheriff into the small office behind the front desk.

"This is the most awful thing that has ever happened. Well, almost." He thought back to an incident a few years back that didn't tarnish the hotel particularly although it unsettled him.[1]

"When did you leave this morning?"

---

1. See THE GIRL ON THE DOORSTEP

"Greg and I had to get some supplies in town and, as it was the staff's half day, we took whoever wanted to spend the day in Pittsfield."

"Not the porter?"

"No. He said he wanted to stay and enjoy the quiet."

"Did you think that was odd?"

"He was an odd sort of fellow. Just turned up a few weeks ago, said he was hitchhiking from Canada back to Mexico and needed a job."

"Did he say, 'back to' Mexico?"

"Yes. It's not unusual to get folks in the summer, young people mostly, who are traveling and in need of some cash who agree to stay a few weeks, sometimes the entire season. They've done this kind of work before, and Tony assured me he had worked in a hotel in Montreal and knew how to wait tables and haul luggage—well, that doesn't take any more skill than a strong back and a willingness to work. But he was secretive. No, that's not the term I was looking for. He was quiet, always observing everyone. Like taking notes in his mind of what people were doing."

"Do you think he was up to some scheme?"

"I can't say. It was just a feeling."

"But you had words with him about something?"

"I'm not proud that I lost my temper."

Daniels allowed the silence to continue until George was compelled to speak. "He was talking to my daughter-in-law in a fashion that I thought was flirtatious." He looked away.

"Did she seem uncomfortable?"

"She laughed at whatever he said. And, no, I didn't hear what it was that he said, but I still didn't like it. He'd never have done that if Greg were in the room."

They heard a car approaching the front doors and George left the office to see that an ambulance had parked outside. Two attendants exited and came into the lobby carrying a folded stretcher and looked around trying to figure out who to talk to. George and Greg stepped forward to show them the way to the kitchen while the Sheriff followed to make sure things were done properly.

Louisa sighed and put her head on Rob's shoulder. "This is so awful. Can we leave in the morning?"

"That might not be possible," Brendan said. "I'm sure the Sheriff will want to talk to each of us."

As they waited with their eyes directed at the hallway, the front doors opened again, and Professor Dalrymple and his wife came in, accompanied by a gust of wind.

"Is something the matter?" he asked, but no one answered as the attendants were returning with the sheet-covered body between them.

Greg scurried around in front of them to open the two sets of doors and stood outside until they secured their cargo in the back and drove away.

"Oh, no!" Mrs. Dalrymple said, looking around the room at who wasn't there and sank into a chair. "Poor Mr. Rostov!"

"What about him?" the Sheriff asked. "And who are you?"

"These are the Dalrymples," George said.

"Where is this Rostov?" Daniels asked.

"He's probably in his room. He has a cast on his leg, which makes navigation on crutches difficult. Jimmy made him a box lunch this morning since he knew he'd be out most of the day."

"Who was that, then?" Professor Dalrymple asked, gesturing to the front doors.

"Tony," George answered.

As they still seemed puzzled, he added, "The porter."

"Where have you two been?" the Sheriff asked.

"We took a drive to see some of surrounding countryside and had lunch in Pittsfield."

Daniels grunted and asked Brendan to step down the hall for a moment. He followed with some surprise until they were out of earshot of the others in the lobby.

"Look, this is unusual, but I have no backup and I'm stepping a bit out of the lines when I say this, but I do need help getting through interviews with everyone. That doesn't mean you're entirely in the clear yet, but…"

"What do you mean? I didn't even know the man except he brought our bags upstairs and I gave him a tip. And I discovered the body!"

"That last bit doesn't eliminate you." Daniels sighed and pinched his lower lip between his fingers as he thought. "We have to interview everybody, but there are some who can be eliminated almost at once since so many of you were out of the building."

Brendan hesitated. "Sure, I can help."

"Thank you," the Sheriff said and shook Brendan's hand.

"By the way, do you have some kind of identification?"

The telephone rang at the front desk, a jarring noise in the otherwise silent lobby. Greg went to the phone and nodded and said, "Yes." He picked up his coat slung across the lobby's desk and said to his father, "I'll be picking up the rest of the crew now."

No sooner had he left than John Taylor pulled up and dashed inside.

"I heard an ambulance was dispatched to the hotel and passed it on the road. What's going on?" His thoughts of someone being ill were erased when he recognized Sheriff Daniels emerging from the gloom of the hallway.

"Who is it?"

"One of the staff. Tony Rivers."

"I spoke with him yesterday," John said, stunned at the news. With his coat still on, he sat down next to Aggie and put his head in his hands. "Just yesterday."

Chapter 9

"What room is Mr. Rostov in?" the Sheriff asked George and, getting the information, he and Brendan took the elevator up.

A knock on the door was met with the answer, "Come. The door is unlocked."

They stopped in the entry and saw the occupant lying in bed with his right foot in its cast resting on a pillow.

"I'm sorry," the man said in accented British English. "Please sit down. I learned there has been an incident in the hotel."

"Who told you?"

"Just now, my good friend, Mrs. Browne came to tell me. I do have crutches but am not very clever with them, so I appreciated that she let me know. I assume you are Sheriff Daniels?"

"Yes, and this is Detective Halloran of the Boston Police assisting me in this matter."

"Oh—was it someone important who died that it brings such expertise to bear?"

He smiled and smoothed down his pencil moustache.

"It was the porter, Tony."

"I do not know the gentleman," Rostov said.

"May we sit down?" the Sheriff asked.

"Pardon my manners. Of course," he gestured to the two armchairs in the room.

"That looks nasty," Daniels said, nodding at the elevated leg.

"Someone suggested I wear these ridiculous golf pants for ease of dressing. And I apologize for the hideous socks, as well," Rostov said, pointing to the vivid argyle pattern that covered his left leg entirely and only the foot of the right.

"I was referring to the cast," Daniels clarified.

Rostov closed his eyes and shook his head. "Of course. I slipped on the ice and here I am."

"Why are you here?" the Sheriff asked.

"It happened in town where I was doing some business. By coincidence, I heard that Mrs. Browne would be staying here, and I hired a car to bring me up so I could recuperate in some congenial company at least."

"What luck," Daniels said.

"It's very quiet here and I have plenty to read." He gestured to a pile of books on the nightstand.

"Have you been in your room all day?"

"I went down for breakfast and spoke to the chef—his name is Jimmy, I believe—and asked if he could prepare a lunch to be brought to my room later. To save me the effort of trying to walk. He told me the staff would be gone most of the day but agreed to make something right then that one of the maids would bring up. An American favorite: ham and cheese sandwich."

Daniels and Brendan looked over at the small table near the window and could see the remains of crusts partly covered with a cloth napkin.

"With the exception of my morning visit downstairs, I have been here the whole time. Not only is it cumbersome to move around with those crutches, but my leg also still hurts underneath the cast. I was not expecting that."

"How much longer will it be on?" Brendan asked.

"At least four more weeks. Mrs. Browne has offered to put me up for the remainder of my recuperation at her home in Boston."

"That will be nice. Most of my party is from Boston," Brendan said.

"Yes, so I was told."

"Did the porter come up to your room at any time?"

"Today? Not at all. He brought up my bags when I first got here, of course. One of the women delivered the sandwich. While I spoke to Mrs. Browne, who came to my room, I haven't had any visitors."

Daniels stood up. "Well, thank you, Mister Rostov. I'll be coming and going until we get a better idea of what occurred here."

They shook hands all around and left the invalid in his bed.

Once they were down the hall, Daniels said, "I also learned where this Tony's room was from George. Why don't we take a look around?"

They took the elevator and, when they exited, immediately noticed how much colder it was.

"One of our party suggested that the Fosters might heat the guest rooms but be less generous about the staff rooms," Brendan said.

It was eerily quiet with all the staff out of the building and the usual clanking of steam heat radiators absent.

"It's this one," the Sheriff said, opening a door to a darkened room. He went to the sole window and gave the shade a jerk, and it popped up to the top with a puff of dust. There was frost on the outside and the inside edges of the windowpane. "It's going to be dark soon." He turned back to see that Brendan was already looking in the closet and finding very little in the way of clothing, just a pair of shoes and a duffel bag on the floor. He took it out and put it on the bed.

The Sheriff was busy opening the drawers of the chest one by one and moving socks and shirts aside to see if anything was underneath.

"Pretty clean. Let's check the bed." He moved the duffel bag onto the floor, looked under the bed, pulled the mattress back from the top to the bottom and, finding nothing, hoisted the duffel bag back onto the bedspread.

Brendan reached in and detailed what he pulled out. "Maps, address book, pad of paper, sweater and that's it.

Where's his passport? If he was traveling from Mexico to the States and Canada and back again, he should have one."

"They're not so picky at the Canadian border about Yanks coming over. I don't know about Mexico, though."

With everything emptied out of the duffel bag, Brendan put one hand on the outside and the other inside and patted the sides and the bottom. "What's this?" he said as he encountered something in the bottom wedged between the lining and the exterior. Using his fingers, he poked and pulled out a United States passport.

"Anthony Rivers," he said, holding it up so Daniels could see the photograph.

"That looks like our guy. South to Mexico and up to Canada in the past year."

"George said that some of the temporary help are young people on a cross-country trip out to see the world or students in the summertime saving for college tuition. This guy was in his thirties. Likely not a student."

"I wonder if his accent was an affectation. John said they had a brief conversation in Spanish."

"Who was this guy? What was he doing here? And who wanted to kill him?" Daniels asked aloud. "And where did the gun come into it?"

"Ah, the gun. Once you get the prints off it, we might know more. But from what I understand, Hextilda Browne was toting a gun in her handbag."

"What!"

"She has this notion that her daughter is in danger of being kidnapped as you heard. That's why they're here in the first place. Although if she wanted to hide out, how strange is it that she should tell Rostov of her plans to come here. I wonder how she knows him?"

Daniels groaned.

"We should search all the rooms, but not now. I want to talk to the staff when they get back and if I'm here any longer, Foster is going to have to feed me dinner. Let's circle back to Mrs. Browne and see what she has to say about her gun."

They took the elevator down to the floor with the guest rooms, glad of the additional warmth, and knocked on Caroline and Hextilda's door. The older woman was up and about, dressed in preparation for cocktail hour by the looks of it, with no visible trace of illness. Caroline was sitting at the table reading a book.

"Hello again," Hextilda said.

"Feeling better?" Daniels asked.

"Yes, ever so much better. Rest is always the cure."

"I just had a few more questions. How do you know Mr. Rostov?"

"Oh, I can't remember who made the introductions, but someone from my Boston circle. He wants me to help him write a book."

"About what?"

"He's Russian, you know. Aristocracy and all that. I must have commented about how fascinating his life had been growing up in Saint Petersburg and a country estate, the people that he knew and the difficult life he has had since then. One thing led to another, and the subject of a memoir came about."

"Are you an author?" Daniels asked.

"Yes, but I mostly write fiction."

Brendan caught Caroline's sardonic smile as this was said.

"Well, thank you," the Sheriff said, exiting with Brendan. Back in the elevator he said, "I want to talk to Jimmy."

"Do you already know him?"

"Yes, he's from a local family. As is Olive."

"You must find it hard to believe that people you know could be capable of murder."

"Sorry to say, but the only murder cases I've had before involved family members pushed to the brink. I can't recall even hearing about an outsider being killed in this county. Not that we have many outsiders. Except for that one girl. That's another story."

Brendan didn't seek details but thought he might ask John for some information about the community later. They made their way to the kitchen, now bustling with activity and noise. Jimmy, in his chef's whites spooning batter into a large pan at the prep table, looked up at the entry of the two men.

"Sheriff," he nodded.

"This is Detective Halloran. A guest who is also helping me out."

"I hope you've enjoyed the food so far."

"Yes, it's been wonderful."

"What's that?" the Sheriff asked.

"Cornbread. Staff's half-day dinner menu is aways simple. Tonight is chili and cornbread." He paused. "This thing with Tony is shocking. Who would do such a thing?"

His meaty face was lined with concern.

"Was there any friction between Tony and the other folks working here?"

"Nah," he said. "Everybody seems to get along fine. He was a pretty quiet guy, didn't share much about himself. Except that he had come down from Canada. I don't know why he planned on staying on through the winter season. You'd think he'd want to go somewhere warmer." He hoisted the large pan off the table and onto the top of the huge stove before opening the oven and sliding it in.

"Did he talk about family at all?"

Jimmy shrugged his large shoulders. "You need to find next of kin, right?"

"It would be helpful. But maybe impossible. Say, where were you today?" the Sheriff asked, although he already knew.

"Got dropped in Pittsfield for the day. Got a few things, went to my parents' house for lunch."

"You don't have a car up here?"

"No. I'm giving my car a rest for the winter while I'm up here. With three meals a day to prepare basically by myself, I don't have the time to be driving back and forth to town. I've got a room upstairs and that suits me fine."

"Sounds kind of lonely," Brendan said.

"Not too bad. I'm saving up to buy a farm."

"Why didn't Tony go into town with you?"

"He didn't say. He kept himself to himself and maybe he wanted to be alone. Gee, you think if he had come with us, it wouldn't have happened? Do you think it was a robbery that went bad?"

"That's what we aim to figure out. I'll talk to George and see if anything was taken from the office. By the way, did Tony get along with the owners?"

"I guess. He did what he was told with no back talk. Didn't complain, either."

"Thanks, Jimmy."

Daniels stopped outside in the hallway and turned to Brendan. "Maybe it was a robbery. We didn't find any money in his room. But how much would he possibly have had? Let's talk to George again."

They found George in the office behind the lobby desk, and he asked them to sit down. "Are you getting any answers on this?" he asked.

"Early days. Have you checked to see if anything may have been stolen?"

"First thing. Whoever did this probably didn't come into this room or, if they did, there's no trace. I keep minimal cash here and I just went to the bank today to deposit what was in the safe."

"When is payday for the staff?"

"It was yesterday. I do that so they have cash for their half-day for whatever they need it for or to put in the bank."

"We didn't find any money in Tony's room or in his pockets. What do you think happened?"

"I don't know who could have taken it. Maybe he hid it? It couldn't have been one of my folks—they went to town with us."

"What if someone stole it from his room? He was found down here in the kitchen. Maybe he never went back upstairs."

"I was too busy getting things together to go to town to notice who was where. You all left before we did," George said to Brendan.

"That's true. Some of the staff were sitting in the lobby waiting to go, but I wasn't familiar with who was who or how many of them there were," Brendan said. "I was too busy maneuvering the skis on my shoulder. Oh, wait—it was Tony who brought the skis and poles out from a storage room towards the back patio and into the lobby for us to carry out to the car." The thought that he had been one of the last to see the man alive was jarring. "But why shot?"

"That, my good detective, is what I hope to find out after I dust the weapon when I get back tonight. I don't have any high hopes that there are prints on it, but you never know. I'll see you all tomorrow. Brendan, please let folks know to stay here so we can talk to them."

"I'll bet Caroline will plead that she's already given you her alibi and wants to go skiing."

"Well, let her. Her mother's not going anywhere. Nor our Russian friend. With that, I'll say good evening," the Sheriff said.

"I thought you were going to stay for dinner?"

"Chili is not my thing," he said, touching his stomach.

Chapter 10

Brendan went to his room to find Rob seated at the table near the window reading the local newspaper that the staff had brought back from town.

"How did it go?" he asked in his usual mild manner.

"I'm bushed. First from my stunted attempt at skiing and then trudging around the hotel, talking to this person and that."

"No progress?"

"None. The Sheriff wants everyone to stay here tomorrow morning for interviews. I can't imagine it will take long. After all, we were all at the ski lodge."

"Except for Caroline."

"True. But I can't think she knew Tony."

"What about the kidnap threat you told me about?"

"I don't know how real that is or if it's Hextilda exaggerating. We'll need for her to be more specific. Was it a letter?

Or a telephone call threat? If Rostov—the man with the cast—knew that Mrs. Browne was going to be here, surely someone else must have known. She's not particularly close-mouthed about things."

Rob laughed. "It's something that rubs Caroline the wrong way. Neither she nor Fred share any information with her if they can help it. You've heard the expression, 'tele-gram, tele-phone and tele-browne'."

Brendan shook his head. "I'm taking a bath," he said. "A good hot soak always hits the spot. By the time I'm a prune, the dinner gong will have sounded."

He didn't get to soak very long before there was a loud shriek from down the hall that propelled him out of the bath and hastily into a bathrobe. When he opened the door, he could see that Rob had left and was halfway down the hall from where the screams were coming.

Rob pounded on the door and Caroline hastily opened it to a scene with her mother on the bed, her handbag open and her hands to her face.

"What's going on?" Rob asked.

"It's gone!" the older woman said.

Brendan appeared at that moment, in a bathrobe, his hair wet, barefoot and water streaming down his legs.

"What?"

"My gun!" She calmed down a bit and clarified. "It was my husband's gun," she said as if that explained everything.

"So, you weren't exaggerating about her bringing a weapon here," Brendan said to Caroline.

Footsteps behind him indicated that the other residents of the floor—Aggie, John, Amanda and Louisa—had also heard the noise and had come to investigate.

"When was the last time you saw it?" Brendan asked.

"Last night. It was in my handbag during dinner. I didn't leave the room this morning, except for a foray downstairs at one point, so I didn't take my handbag with me. That means someone must have come into our room last night, Caroline. While we were sleeping!" She let out a groan of horror. "We could have been killed in our beds."

"Mother, calm down."

"Did someone take the bullets, too?" Brendan asked.

"I don't know." She opened a small jewelry box that was on top of the chest of drawers. "No."

"Was the gun loaded?" Brendan asked.

"Of course! What's the good of having a gun if it's not ready to be used?"

THAT EVENING the level of conversation in the living room was subdued and Eunice and Olive were like robots performing their tasks.

"What can they be feeling right now?" Amanda asked. "Tony's death seems so senseless."

"There's that, and the fact that nothing was stolen. Except maybe a week's pay," Brendan said.

"Do you think Hextilda's gun was the murder weapon?"

"We might know by tomorrow."

They ate in silence for a few minutes before Aggie changed the subject. "John, how is Mrs. Parsons?"

"Who is that?" Caroline asked.

"A patient of his who fell. It's why he dashed off to Pittsfield. That's right—you weren't at the lodge when all that happened. We were afraid we might have left you behind."

"I wasn't doing too well myself and wrenched my knee. I told the Sheriff that I hitched a ride back with someone who was leaving."

"Who was that?" Brendan asked.

"Somebody named Bob." She shrugged her shoulders. "Lives nearby."

Amanda looked at Brendan through half-closed eyes.

Caroline looked at her mother and Mr. Rostov across the room deep in conversation and hardly aware of anyone else. She got up abruptly and walked over to her mother, said a few words, then returned to the table where the three couples sat and said, "I've got a devil of a headache. I'm going to bed." And she left the dining room, hardly limping.

"Good," Louisa said once the other woman was out of earshot. "Now we can talk about all of this without feeling strange."

"All what?" Aggie asked.

"This business about a kidnap attempt. It sounds entirely made up to me. Just trying to attract attention to herself," Louisa said.

"I don't think we know enough about it," Amanda said. "Maybe the whole thing was in Hextilda's imagination."

John shook his head. "I know she seems batty sometimes, but you can't think she made the whole thing up, can you?"

"She makes up entire novels out of thin air!" Louisa said.

"I'd like to know exactly what she heard or saw to jump to such a conclusion," Brendan said.

"It must have been something significant. I mean, if I suspected something like that was afoot, I would call the police," Amanda said. "And not run out of town with a loaded gun in my handbag."

"Of course. That could have gone off at any moment. Remember her sort of slamming her handbag down on the table last night?"

The Dalrymples were seated far enough away not to be able to overhear them, but the three couples kept their conversation at a low level anyway.

"Do you think any of the folks who were away for the day might have doubled back and committed the crime?" Amanda asked.

"The Tweeds said they were sightseeing but made no comment about what they saw. There's something off about that woman," Louisa said. She reduced her voice to a whisper. "Her hair for one thing. It looks like a bad wig."

"Louisa!" Amanda said more loudly than she intended, and Professor Dalrymple looked over at their table and nodded with a smile.

"Honestly, Louisa. Perhaps it's a wig because she has thinning hair."

"Her husband ought to get her a better one."

"Academics don't make as much money as everyone supposes," Rob said. "I don't mind the students coming into the Oasis because they're spending Daddy's money. But the early afternoon history faculty members from Boston University are notorious for nursing one beer over the course of an hour."

There was a loud crash from the kitchen and a man's raised voice, then a slammed door. All the diners looked at one another but otherwise kept eating. A few minutes later, the two waitresses who also served as the maids in the off-season came in to offer beverage refills or clear plates. Eunice had her mouth in a firm line and looked as if she had been crying.

After they had left, Amanda asked Brendan what he and Daniels would be doing the next day.

"It may seem ridiculous, but we have to interview everyone, including those of us at this table."

"But why?" Louisa asked. "We were all skiing and have each other for alibis."

"I know that sounds legitimate, but just as the suggestion was made that those who were away for the day could have doubled back, one of us could have done the same. Myself excluded since I was in lessons until noon and the instructor can vouch for the fact. You all…"

"Don't be ridiculous," Louisa said. "I didn't even know the porter's name. And we all saw one another throughout the morning. Except John," she added in all seriousness.

"I know. I was doing backcountry runs," he said.

Aggie looked at him with concern.

"All by myself. And no, I did not shoot the porter."

Their waitress, Olive, came to the table and let Brendan know there was a telephone call for him at the front desk.

"It's Daniels," the Sheriff said when Brendan picked up the phone. "No prints on the gun. Not surprised. But the bullet matches the gun. That narrows things down considerably."

"In terms of people, but in terms of motive?"

The Sheriff said nothing.

"I didn't mention this before, but the scene was contaminated in more ways than one," Brendan said. "When I took the Fosters into the kitchen, George knocked a glass of water onto the prep table and mopped it up with a towel before I could do anything. If there were fingerprints on the table, he did a good job of rubbing them out. Then as we saw, Jimmy was in the kitchen later preparing dinner working on the same table."

The Sheriff sighed. "I don't think Jimmy had anything to do with it. George had a bit of a beef with Tony, however. He told me he thought the porter was flirting with his daughter-in-law."

"Who is that?"

"Eunice. She's one of the waitresses or maids or whatever they are calling themselves. In any case, see you tomorrow."

Chapter 11

Sheriff Daniels arrived early the next morning as everyone was coming down for the buffet breakfast. George greeted him in the lobby and pressed him to have something to eat.

"The wife got me sorted this morning. But I will have some coffee with the detective, if you don't mind."

"Go right ahead."

Daniels spotted Brendan about to sit down with a full plate of food with his friends and asked him to go to a separate table with him. "Just to chart out the day," he added.

"Please, dig in." He poured himself a cup of coffee from the carafe on the table and said, "I know you and your people are here on vacation, and I want to get this cleared up as quickly as possible. My thought is to interview your party this morning and get that out of the way. At first glance, it doesn't seem like any of you could possibly be involved."

"I agree most heartily with you on that."

"We still must confirm it. Too bad it's interrupted your ski holiday."

"It was my first attempt and all I got out of it was a diminished ego, cold feet and sore legs. The others are veterans, and I wouldn't like to take away from their time any more than you would. We can start as soon as I finish eating."

"Good man," Daniels said and savored the rich coffee so different from what he was used to at home.

When he was done, Brendan explained to the others the plan for the morning. Luckily, Caroline had not come downstairs yet, because she would not be included in the guests who would be so quickly dismissed. They agreed enthusiastically, and he proposed that the interviews take place in the library and suggested that Amanda be first.

"I detect preferential treatment," Louisa said with a smile.

"Absolutely," her sister agreed. Amanda, Brendan and the Sheriff went down the hallway to the cozy room whose radiator was keeping it at a reasonable temperature.

"Now, tell me everything you know about the porter," Daniels asked.

"Everything I know is hearsay from the rest of the group. I know he carried our bags upstairs and Brendan gave him a tip. And that's all."

"Did you speak to him?"

"Not at all. I may have smiled in appreciation, but we didn't have a conversation."

"Did he seem to have an accent?"

"As I said, we didn't talk to one another, so I couldn't say."

"What were your movements yesterday morning."

"We went in two cars to the lodge, bought our lift tickets and took the tow rope to the top of the mountain. We skied until about noon, when we had agreed to have lunch."

"Did you see the others during this time?"

"I didn't see Brendan. He was off with the instructor. John disappeared into the trees, but I saw Louisa and Aggie and went down the mountain with them many times."

"How about Rob and Caroline."

"Oh, yes, Rob joined us and Caroline on the first run and then she said she would catch up after she adjusted her bindings. We saw Rob from time to time—he took more difficult runs that we did. From then on, we must have been on a different schedule with Caroline. She was going up as we were coming down and vice versa."

"Did you see her? Or are you just assuming that was the case?"

"That's a good question. I didn't see her until we got back to the hotel. I just thought she had continued skiing, and we wondered where she was when we all met up for lunch."

"Anything else you would like to add?"

"No. I had minimal contact with the porter so I'm afraid I can be of little help."

"Brendan, any questions for the lady?"

"No. I think she's clean. But you may not know that she is a private detective and may be able to assist in some way."

Amanda narrowed her eyes at him but said, "Of course, I could assist. But I think you two professionals have it under control." She stood, shook hands with both men and turned to leave. "If you need my help with any of the others, yes, I'd like to listen in at the least."

"Oh, wait. Could you ask Louisa to come in?" Brendan asked.

"Yes, sir," she replied, giving him a little salute.

Louisa came in, sat down and immediately looked at her wristwatch. She was already dressed for a ski day in a colorful, thick wool sweater and sat on the edge of her chair as if to leap up at a moment's notice. She put on her most charming smile waiting for the first question.

"Where were you yesterday morning?"

Louisa looked at Brendan. "After I left here, we went to the ski lodge. Brendan knows, he was with me."

"And did you stay there all morning?"

"Yes."

"Can anyone vouch for you?"

"I should think so. First of all, my sister. And then my boyfriend, Rob. We went down several runs together."

"Did you leave the ski area during any point in the morning?"

"Of course not. There was nowhere to go except by car and I didn't have the keys. We stopped for lunch, John Taylor was summoned to the phone and left to go back to the hotel, and Brendan decided to call it a day. We were midway through the meal when Brendan called up there and we hustled back here."

"Did you talk to the porter at all?"

"No. Not a bit. He carried up our luggage and Rob gave him a tip. That was the extent of my interaction with the man. Are we done here?" She started to get up.

"You're good friends with Caroline, isn't that right?"

"Yes," she answered hesitantly, as if stepping into an uncomfortable conversation.

"What do you know about a kidnapping attempt?"

"Nothing, really, except that she said her mother thought it was valid and that's why Hextilda whisked her away to this place."

"Didn't you think that was odd?" the Sheriff persisted.

"Of course. That's the sort of person Mrs. Browne is. Unpredictable, volatile."

"As in quick to anger?"

"No, I didn't mean to imply that. Just that she is prone to flights of fancy, I would say."

"So, she made it all up? For what purpose?"

"I don't know. Why don't you ask her?" Louisa could feel the minutes ticking away while the Sheriff asked questions to which she had no answers.

"What is so special about Caroline?"

Louisa sputtered, seeking an appropriate response. "If you're to believe her mother, enemies of the Guzmán family are lying in wait to destroy them, and getting to them through her daughter would be the best way."

"Do you agree?"

"I have no idea how real that danger is, if it exists at all. But I think we've exhausted all the information I can provide, unless you'd like to ask me for a forecast of spring fashions." She got up.

"Thank you, Miss Burnside. It's been a pleasure."

Brendan had his head bent over his notebook so she couldn't see his smile.

"Would you mind asking Mr. Worley to come in?"

She turned on her heel and left abruptly.

"Hello, Mr. Worley," the Sheriff greeted him.

"Rob. I'm glad to see you're still in one piece," he said to Brendan with a chuckle.

"Can you detail the events of yesterday morning?"

"Breakfast here, then we piled into two cars with our gear and went up to the lodge for what we thought was the day."

"I understand the gear was stowed down here somewhere rather than in your rooms?"

"Yes, as we were unloading the cars when we first got here, the porter first took our luggage upstairs and then he left. I assumed it was he who put everything in a closet or storeroom. Were you with him, Brendan?"

"No, he did it on his own unless the Fosters helped him. I

did see which room he put it in, though. With six of us, there was quite a lot of stuff to lug around," he answered.

"Did you notice anything amiss with the man?"

"No, but my interaction with him was so limited, I wouldn't know what his usual demeanor was." He brushed a speck of lint off his wool ski pants, looked up at the Sheriff and smiled.

Daniels was struck with the man's poise as well as his all-American good looks.

"Some folks have mentioned that he had an accent. Did you notice?"

"To be honest, I had so few words with him that I couldn't tell. He said 'all right' about storing the gear and 'okay' when I told him and 'thank you' when I gave him a tip. That's not much to go on."

"Were you in sight of the others yesterday at the ski resort?"

Rob looked over at Brendan. "He was holed up with an instructor, out of sight. We were on the main runs, which I did with Louisa, Amanda and Aggie."

"Where was John Taylor?" the Sheriff asked, looking concerned.

"He decided to go off-piste and was tackling areas where there are no groomed runs. But that seems to be the nature of the man."

"Yes, that sounds like the good doctor," Daniels agreed. "I've known him since he arrived here."

"But I was with the Burnside sisters and their cousin and at the beginning with Caroline, but she seemed to get out of synch with our rhythm. We agreed to meet at lunch, which we did. We couldn't locate Caroline and were about to eat until John got called away for some medical emergency."

"Yes, I heard about that."

"It was then that I got a ride back to the hotel with him, having had enough for one day," Brendan said. "And you know the rest."

"What do you know of a kidnap attempt on Caroline?"

"Nothing other than she mentioned at dinner that her mother thought she was in danger. Caroline seemed to make light of it."

"That's all, I think, Rob. Could you ask John to come in? Thank you." They shook hands and the Sheriff and Brendan had a few minutes to confer.

"We don't seem to be getting any new information. I suppose it's just a matter of form that we're doing these interviews," Daniels said.

It occurred to Brendan that the Sheriff might not have gone to all this trouble if he hadn't been there. Perhaps he thought this is how the Boston Police worked, and he needed to go through the laborious task of asking everybody the same questions for the purpose of seeming thorough. Well, it was his case. Let him do what he wanted to do.

John came in, his large frame and presence filling the room.

"Glad to be of help, but I don't think I know very much that's going to help you."

"You never know. Tell me about your morning yesterday."

John recounted his actions, the backcountry adventure and meeting the rest of the party for lunch, only to receive a call to head back to Pittsfield. He added that he had no notion that anything was wrong at the hotel until he overheard that an ambulance had been sent to the Mountain Aire and, being concerned, he came back as quickly as possible.

"Did you have much interaction with the porter?" the Sheriff asked.

"No, but possibly more than the others. I picked up his accent when we first arrived and the syntax of one sentence when he spoke, which told me he was not a native speaker of English. I tried out a Spanish phrase on him and we began to talk."

At last, the Sheriff thought. *Somebody may know something.*

"Assuming that he came from Central or South America, I asked him how he liked the weather up here. He smiled and moved his head from side to side, indicating he wasn't going to commit himself to liking it or not. I asked him how long he had been here and he said, 'not long.' I chatted on, hoping he would respond in kind just to be friendly. I couldn't place his accent, and he seemed reluctant to talk more than necessary, so I left it at that."

"And what other interactions did you have with him?"

"Aside from that when we first arrived, I only saw him in the dining room, helping to wait on the tables. The women evidently were assigned our large table, and he must have been assigned the Dalrymples and Mr. Rostov. When Mrs. Browne turned and saw him, she was startled."

"What do you mean?"

"She seemed frightened and, because of that, one of the waitresses took over for him."

"Do you know why she reacted that way?"

"It may be that she was so engrossed in her conversation with her dinner partner and whatever they were discussing that she was startled by the interruption. She joined our table after Mr. Rostov went upstairs, and she didn't explain her behavior to us. Just rattled along about him and his difficulties. I have met her before, and I noticed that she likes to get her son and daughter on edge."

The Sheriff blinked his eyes. "Whatever for?"

John shrugged. "To get attention? I don't know. It's not how anyone in my family behaves. She suggested she might bring the man back to Boston and let him stay at their home, which, of course, got Caroline up in arms."

"I don't understand. Why should her daughter be upset?"

John laughed. "I understand Mrs. Browne lives in a large house in Beacon Hill. However, her daughter and her husband live there, too, as well as Mrs. Browne's son and soon-to-be daughter-in-law."

"I grew up with four brothers and sisters. We fit six of us at a kitchen table without a problem and doubled up in the bedrooms," Daniels said.

"So did I," Brendan chimed in. "But you're dealing with a different ilk. I ought to know."

John laughed. "I married into the down-to-earth branch of the family. You know, Caroline's behavior reminds me of when you have a dog and then take in a stray. There's bound to be jealousy and resentment. Those are my two cents for psychology."

Daniels shook his head, not fully comprehending the Brownes' situation.

"Caroline told us before she left after dinner that her mother had brought a gun for protection," John added.

The Sheriff stood up and put his hands in his pockets. "I've had just about enough of those folks being so vague. After I talk to Aggie and you all go skiing, I'm going to try to pin down that woman again about the supposed kidnap threat." He shooed John out of the room. "And please tell your lovely wife that we're ready to talk to her."

Aggie promptly appeared at the library door, looking ready to say what she knew and get going for the day.

"Well, Sheriff, I wish I had information and theories to impart, but I really don't." When she smiled, the resemblance to her cousin Amanda was striking.

"That may be true, but sometimes there's a little nugget hidden away."

"Fire away!"

"Please describe your interactions with the porter, Tony."

"He carried our bags to our room and I listened while John spoke to him in Spanish and, after a tip was provided, he left. I'm afraid that's the sum of it. I didn't speak to him at all."

"That's disappointing."

CHRISTMAS MURDER ON THE SLOPES

"I saw him in the dining room waiting on tables, but as is common, you tend to overlook the servers, especially if you're involved in lively company with a lot of conversation."

The Sheriff was disappointed, knowing that Aggie had in the past shown a keen eye for observation and deduction. "That's all?"

"About him, yes. But I can tell you that I am acquainted with Mrs. Browne, having spent a brief time at her place in Vermont.[13] She's quite dramatic as she recounts events, and I sometimes fear they are more in her imagination than reality. If that sounds that I haven't given specifics, that's intentional."

The Sheriff was surprised at the comment, and it intrigued him enough that he was about to press her, but she held up a finger and shook her head.

"Time to go skiing," she said.

"Thank you. Can you ask the Dalrymples to come in on your way through the lobby?"

Daniels jotted down a few more notes while he waited for one or the other of the couple to come into the library. Instead, Aggie came back alone.

"They've gone into town. With Mr. Rostov and Mrs. Browne."

"Drat!"

---

1. [3] See COUNTRY HOUSE CHRISTMAS MURDER

"In that case, I'll catch up with the others and put myself to the test again with the instructor. I'm graduating to the tow rope today," Brendan said.

Chapter 12

Despite the recent murder at the hotel, the group was determined to enjoy what they could from their vacation together. Caroline rode with Aggie and John, and the other two couples were packed into Rob's car. As it was getting toward the weekend, there were more cars in the parking lot and people on the slopes. The day was overcast, suggesting a snowstorm on the way.

"We could be in luck and get a fresh covering of powder by early afternoon," Rob said. "The runs won't be so packed down and slippery then."

Brendan looked at Amanda. "Slippery?" he asked.

"Well, snow is frozen water after all. Isn't that the point?"

"I'm actually quite good at ice skating," Brendan said. "Maybe I should have stuck to that."

"I didn't know that. We'll have to go to Boston Common and take a few spins around the Frog Pond. I can't do anything fancy like spins and jumps, but I can skate backwards." Amanda laughed at the idea. "I haven't been skating in years, however."

"At last, something I may be better at than you," he teased.

Once they got their skis on and poled over to Aggie and John's car, Caroline took Amanda aside.

"Did you happen to see my mother after breakfast? She didn't come back to the room and was acting peculiar."

Amanda stifled the urge to inquire how one would know the difference. "I saw her at the front desk before you came down. She and Mister Rostov wanted to hire a car to go into town. The Dalrymples said they had their car and would be happy to give them a lift as they were headed there themselves."

"Oh, no. What's she up to?"

IT WAS A JOLLY foursome that navigated the winding roads into Pittsfield and Mrs. Dalrymple was particularly animated. Although she was dressed in the same somber tweed suit and long brown coat that aged her terribly, her voice was girlish with excitement.

"We haven't had a proper vacation since the summer. And that was only a weekend on Cape Cod."

"I would think that you'd have the summers off, working at a girls' school," Hextilda said.

Mrs. Dalrymple gave a pained smile. "They only provide living quarters for us during the term. If we want year-round accommodation, Alvan signs on for the summer sessions. You'd be surprised how many families send their girls away for the entire year."

"That is sad," Hextilda said.

"It was very common among our set, too," Rostov said.

"Weren't you terribly lonely?" she asked.

"We children were all in the same boat. Tutored at home until a certain age then shipped off to get a solid education. I've known nothing else."

Hextilda smiled in admiration of the man who had experienced early luxury, then hardship, penury and exile and now a broken leg. But everything he said was spoken with a thrilling Russian-accented British English, making even his difficulties seem romantic.

"How long have you been teaching at the school?" Hextilda asked.

"Almost twenty long years."

"We've been saving for retirement but have not chosen where we could go. There are so many charming little towns on Cape Cod," Martha said.

"Yes, it's wonderful. Fantastic in the summer and much quieter in the winter. But there are year-round residents, of course. And you're not too far from Boston if you want to come into the city for culture."

"Where can we drop you?" Professor Dalrymple asked, looking at Rostov, who sat in the front seat to accommodate his cast.

"I have to check in with the doctor. I'll point out the building as we get closer. You can drop me off."

"Oh, no, no," Alvan said. "We'll come up with you."

"It won't be very interesting I can assure you."

"It will be warmer than sitting in the car. We'll keep you company in the waiting room."

He was directed to a three-story brick building that listed the offices of lawyers and other professionals in the lobby's directory.

"Luckily this building has an elevator, or it would be a long journey upstairs. We go to the third floor."

The offices hummed with morning activity and they could hear telephones ringing and typewriters going at a swift pace behind the closed doors. A young woman came out of one door, nodded to them and went into a room across the hall.

"This is it," Rostov said, lifting his head up to indicate the next door down with Doctor Thompson in black letters painted on the glass.

Alvan opened the door and held it for the other man before allowing both Martha and Hextilda to come in. It was sparsely furnished, with a reception desk and telephone and four chairs arranged in a semicircle around a coffee table with a few magazines and newspapers. As they sat, the doctor in his white coat emerged from behind one of the doors that looked to be his office and greeted Rostov heartily.

"My goodness. I hope you're not all waiting to see me!"

"No, they've kindly offered to wait."

"I apologize that my nurse wasn't here to greet you. She's out getting a prescription filled for an elderly patient who can't make it into town. Come in, sir," he said to Rostov and opened a door to a room where the others could see the corner of a long table. "I hope you're doing well at the Mountain Aire." The door shut behind them.

"This may sound silly, but one thing that makes a visit to the doctor tolerable is they always have the latest magazines. Although my doctor is an avid fly fisherman, and you wouldn't believe how many magazines there are devoted to the topic. All in racks in his waiting room," Hextilda said.

"I do hope Mr. Rostov is all right. I can't imagine slogging along on crutches, especially on the icy sidewalks," Martha said.

"Let's keep walking to a minimum and make sure we flank him in the event of slipping," her husband said.

"Oh, good idea!" Hextilda said.

They busied themselves perusing the reading materials and listening to the murmuring of conversation behind the examination door.

Hextilda looked at her watch and whispered, "He's been in there almost half an hour. What could the doctor be doing? Certainly not changing the cast?"

"I think not," Alvan said. "Perhaps he's giving him dietary recommendations that would ameliorate the healing process."

"Yes, plenty of calcium to knit those bones back together," Hextilda said. "We must tell the chef at the Mountain Aire. I'll be leaving to go home soon as the danger I perceived has passed." She knocked on the wooden coffee table. "I'm seriously thinking of having him stay at my home in Boston. No offense intended toward this doctor, but there are so many more in the big city. And he can stay in comfort there with company and lively conversation instead of stuck in a hotel in the mountains by himself."

"Isn't that kind of you!" Martha said. "Perhaps I'll break my arm and join you—what a merry group we'll be." She laughed and covered her mouth to hide her prominent front teeth.

"You're welcome anytime. When we get back to the hotel, I'll give you my address so we can keep in touch."

"Although we'll be going back to Albany, which is quite in the other direction. And Martha, you know I can't do without you," Alvan said.

The door to the examination room finally opened and Rostov hobbled out, followed by the doctor. "I look forward to getting out of these ridiculous pants," he said.

"They're rather jaunty," Hextilda said. "Especially with the argyle socks."

"Do men actually wear these things anywhere?" Rostov asked.

"Yes, on the links," she said.

"Where is that?"

"Golf courses. Once you get out of that cast, you'll be perfectly outfitted and must take up golf."

This got a chuckle from the Dalrymples but the doctor intervened.

"He's got at least four more weeks in that contraption. We want to make sure that it's properly healed."

Rostov groaned. "Thank you very much for the visit on short notice," he said to the doctor and thumped out on his crutches through the door that the doctor held open for him. The rest of the party followed and made their slow way to the elevator.

"Where to now?" Hextilda said.

"I need to go to the bank," Rostov said. "Bank of Boston."

"It's just down the street. Are you comfortable walking there?"

"I think it is close enough."

They did flank him on the sidewalk in the event of his slipping or becoming tired, but he was a strong person and propelled himself easily. The Pittsfield branch of the Bank of Boston was a miniature of the main branch in Boston at only two stories high. The ceilings of the ground floor were expansive, the floors marble and the fixtures brass. It was a busy day, the end of the week, and merchants were making deposits while other business owners were making withdrawals for their employees' wages.

"Please sit down," Rostov suggested as he stood in line. Customers in front of him urged him to go forward because of his lack of mobility and he thanked them profusely. He reached into his overcoat to get to a pocket in his suit jacket and took something out that he handed to the clerk. The clerk disappeared to one of the back desks and came back with a large envelope.

Hextilda and the Dalrymples had found seating at the other end of the entrance where they could admire the murals of English settlers to the region exchanging gifts with the natives that were painted on the walls.

"Isn't that beautiful?" Hextilda said. "I always wished I had artistic talent. To be able to paint something like that. And at that scale, too."

"But you are an artist, aren't you?" Martha asked. "You write books, I'm told, and that surely is an artistic creation."

Hextilda laughed. "I suppose so, but my children don't think so. Not highbrow enough for them, even if it pays the bills."

"I'm sorry, I don't think I've read any of your works," Martha said.

"It's quite possible you haven't. It's referred to as 'popular fiction.' I write romances that are a bit spicy, if you take my meaning."

"Oh," Martha said.

"Not highbrow, but very popular, although I wish more lucrative."

"Well, Sergei seems to be done already. That was fast." Alvan stood up and they all proceeded out to the street.

"What now?" Hextilda asked.

"I suggest we have an early lunch as I have a proposition to put before you," Rostov said. "I believe I saw a restaurant just down the street." And saying that, he took off with the other three struggling to keep up with his rapid pace.

He was at the door waiting for one of them to open it and swiftly made his way to one of the empty booths. The owner, surprised at the early customers, came out of the kitchen wiping his hands on a towel.

"Good morning. We're still serving breakfast if you like or lunch?"

Rostov spoke for them, "Just coffee for now and we'll order in a bit."

"Certainly," the man said and went back to the kitchen.

Rostov was seated on the aisle, his leg stretched out with a good view of the kitchen.

Hextilda and Martha chatted about the town and perhaps exploring it later in the afternoon since they would not be skiing.

The owner came out with a large pot of coffee and served them as the cups and saucers were already on the table. He left a pitcher of cream and stood waiting for further instructions.

"Thank you, that is all," Rostov said.

The two women looked at each other quizzically, wondering what this abrupt meeting was about and soon found out.

"I'm going to speak to you now of hardship. There is my personal story of which Mrs. Browne is partly aware. A happy childhood—a privileged childhood—loving family, a wide circle of friends. Happy times before the awful times happened in Russia. I don't think you've had the experience of being torn from your home, all you know and all the values that you hold dear. To experience the paralyzing fear of being taken off in the middle of the night to be killed. Your family debating whether to hide their valuables or try to sell them at a fraction of their worth to get funds to escape."

"We had a country place and that seemed the safest place to be. Or so we thought. We left our house in St. Petersburg, disguised in our simplest clothes, almost certain we would never return. Our servants, once so loyal, had scattered, thinking the revolution would make their lives better. They were soon to be disillusioned."

Rostov stopped for a sip of coffee and his three tablemates glanced at one another as if wondering why he chose to tell this personal story to them on this particular day.

"One of the remaining servants got a wagon and accompanied us out to our country place, nobody thinking to stop and question a peasant driving what appeared to be a load of vegetables out of the city. In reality, it was my family and some valuables that were hidden under a crude blanket, making our bumpy way, fear clutching at our throats, my mother barely able to control her weeping."

"We made it out and faced months in the country without word of what was going on back home. It all seemed chaotic—it *was* chaos. First one person in power, then another. And then they came for the Tsar and his family. At that point, we knew we had no protection whatsoever. And we would not make it through the winter with so little food. We traveled to Novorossiysk on the Black Sea, sailed to Istanbul and slowly made our way to England and tried to resume some sort of life with the assistance of other émigrés. It was a tough existence, and I lost many family members, but I do not want to dwell on that. Instead, I wish to tell you of a rare opportunity to salvage some of that old life and one life in particular."

Hextilda could barely contain her excitement because she had figured out what was coming next.

Rostov looked to the kitchen to make sure the owner was not overhearing their conversation and then leaned in over the table.

"We can get Her Imperial Highness Anastasia out of her miserable existence to a safe place."

There was silence before Alvan said, "But she was killed with her family! Everyone knows that."

"No, my friend," Rostov said. "She was not killed. She fell, wounded, and one of the guards took pity on her and smuggled her out of that basement to a waiting wagon. She was carried to a nearby farm and tended by a humble woman who knew enough of the healing arts and discovered, sewn into her undergarments, diamonds. It was these diamonds that deflected what would have been a mortal wound and saved her life. Her poor, miserable life."

"Does anyone else know of this?" Alvan asked.

"Yes, many of us know but we have been sworn to secrecy."

"And yet, you are sharing this with us," Martha said.

"Because I trust you. I have observed all three of you in different circumstances and know that you can be trusted."

The three companions looked at each other.

"You can trust me," Hextilda said, and the others said the same.

"My mission coming into town today was to retrieve a large sum of money, five thousand dollars, being held for me at the bank." He pulled the large envelope from his suit jacket and carefully opened it and showed the Dalrymples the contents. Martha gasped. He then showed it to

Hextilda, who despite her privileged upbringing, had never seen a sum that large in one place.

"The money is not just for her transportation out of Russia—yes, she is still in the Mother country—but for forged identity papers, passport and, of course, the significant bribes.

Rostov closed the envelope and fastened the clasp.

"Mrs. Browne, I entrust this to you."

"What? Why me?"

"I do not feel safe carrying that much money when enemies can be all around me. I told you that I slipped on the ice when I broke my leg. That is not true. Some thugs accosted me, and they did the damage. An unlikely stranger intervened and saved me from being killed outright. That's why I came out to these mountains. That is why I stay in my room at the Mountain Aire. I dare not go out in public. Even today was a great risk."

His companions were agog at the information.

"What can we do?"

"That is only five thousand dollars, and I need at least five more. I may have to leave the safety of my remote hideout and this small town to go back to the City to raise the rest."

"Do you think that the shooting of the porter had something to do with this?" Hextilda asked.

"How clever you are," Rostov said. "Yes, he was my compatriot, sent here before me to survey the lay of the land. And, also, to protect me. Alas, he failed and gave his life."

"Who shot him?"

"I'm not sure yet. I am in hopes that the Sheriff will find out who the culprit was."

"What more can we do? Shall we go to the police?" Martha asked.

"No, we can't draw further attention to my cause."

"You can't go back to the City," Hextilda said. "You wouldn't be safe there if you're not safe here."

They looked at one another in consternation.

"I'll give you some money," Hextilda said. "I have an account at the Bank of Boston."

"I didn't mean to—"

"No, I insist. After lunch, I'm going next door and taking out the money. It's the least I can do for the poor woman. And you. Imagine, she's been living in penury all these years. Her youth gone, her family gone, her country gone."

Rostov wept opening and Hextilda put her hand out to his.

The Dalrymples looked at each other before Alvan spoke. "I'm willing to donate, too. I'm by no means a royalist, but she has suffered more than anyone should. "I can give you two thousand dollars."

"Alvan," his wife said looking at him fiercely. "I think it has to be five."

"Yes, all right, five. That should get her out."

"I'll make my donation five as well," Hextilda said. "She'll need some money when she gets here. She is coming to the States, isn't she?"

"Not directly. That's too dangerous. She'll be going through Europe first, then to England and then to this country. It has to be done in stages so as not to attract attention. Slowly, carefully."

"I certainly hope that, when she gets here, we can celebrate her liberation at my home in Boston."

With tears still on his cheeks, Rostov said, "When the time comes, and when it is safe, yes, it would be my honor to be there." He took a handkerchief from his pocket and dabbed his eyes. He looked toward the kitchen and snapped his fingers. "Sir, sir, we are ready to order."

Chapter 13

Hextilda looked toward the front of the restaurant as the snow that had started to fall while the foursome began their lunch was coming down harder with each passing minute.

"I don't want to spoil this lovely meal, but we probably ought to get going back to the hotel soon before we get snowed in here."

Rostov turned his head as she pointed and agreed. "But what a shame to break up our charming party."

"We do want to get to the bank before long, as well," Alvan said.

That seemed to change Rostov's mind, and he looked toward the kitchen and snapped his fingers again. The owner, his mouth in a thin line at having a customer summon him in such a manner, managed to put on a smile and, sensing the party was breaking up, brought the bill. There was a tug of war between Alvan and Rostov as to who would pay the bill with Rostov assuming the duty with grace.

"After all, my friends, think of how much you have helped me. And lifted my spirits considerably." He looked over the tab carefully before pulling out one bill and handing it to the owner, who surmised that he was not to keep the change. They waited for him to return before putting on their overcoats and making a slow procession to the front door.

"Look at it coming down," Martha said.

The bank was not too far away and, despite their protests that Rostov should remain in the restaurant's foyer until they returned, he went along with them and sat instead in the bank's lobby alongside Martha.

Alvan and Hextilda went to separate tellers to make their withdrawals, and she was surprised that he concluded his business so quickly. Instead, she was made to wait while the teller consulted a man at a desk in the area behind the teller stations. After a brief conversation, both men came forward and the supervisor introduced himself and asked, "Mrs. Browne?"

"Yes," she said.

"Are you sure you wish to take out quite so much money?"

"Yes, the amount is on the withdrawal slip." She hated that they assumed a woman didn't know the value of money. "I'm sure you handle quite a lot of large transactions all the time."

"Not every day," he answered. "I don't usually ask this, but since you're not a local customer, may I see some identification?"

She was taken aback by the request since she had never been pressed about that before. But then, she usually went to the main branch in Boston where they knew her well. She fished in her handbag and, not having a driver's license, wondered what else would suffice.

"Here is my charge account card at Jordan Marsh and my identification card from the Daughters of the American Revolution."

The man took the two small pieces of paper and saw that the signatures matched the one on the withdrawal slip but still hesitated.

"You can call the main branch and verify that it is me. Just give them a description."

He handed back the pieces of identification and smiled. "That won't be necessary. Where are you staying?"

"The Mountain Aire," she said.

"The Fosters have been long-time customers," he said.

SHE LOOKED toward the large windows at the snowfall. "I think we'd better get going soon before we get stuck in a snowdrift." She managed a small laugh and the man initialed the slip and asked her to wait a moment. It turned out to be some minutes that she stood while the man went back to his desk, retrieved a key and disappeared into a back room. Hextilda turned to her companions who were all seated and gave a shrug as if to indicate she didn't know what was taking so long. The teller was trying not to make eye contact and instead pulled out a drawer and counted some bills putting a rubber band around them.

"Hope we didn't clean you out," she said.

"Oh, no. We're a solid bank, all right."

The manager finally returned with an envelope, took out the bills and counted them discreetly in front of her, then put the money back in the envelope along with a receipt. "Have a Merry Christmas, Mrs. Browne."

"Thank you," she said and the threesome got up and joined her to exit the building.

"Just in time, I think," Alvan said. "My teller said they might close early because of the weather."

"Do you think we should go back to the hotel?" Martha asked.

"What do you propose? Holing up in town here somewhere? Don't be silly. It's coming down fast, but the sidewalk isn't slick, and the roads probably aren't, either." Nonetheless, they moved as quickly as they could, with Rostov breathing heavily from the exertion.

Surprisingly, as they left town, the snowfall abated even as the sun was invisible behind the mountains and they made it safely back to the hotel. The skiing guests had gathered in the lobby because the lodge had closed early for the day due to a whiteout there. A bit disappointed, they were still in their ski clothing, drinking hot cocoa and enjoying the fire.

"What a hearty group!" Hextilda said, seeing them through the window as she stomped the snow off her boots outside the foyer. Going inside, she went up to Caroline and put her hand on her shoulder. "Your cheeks are so rosy from the exercise. Perhaps I ought to take up skiing," she said.

Brendan looked at her and shook his head. "It's quite a bit harder than it looks. Trust me on that."

"You did very well today," Amanda said. "Mastered the tow rope, even did some fancy turns."

"And a few colossal tumbles. A good thing the snow is deep. It's still awkward with sticks strapped onto your feet. I've seen newsreels of ski jumping and, while I was impressed with the derring-do, I can't imagine hurtling down a slippery slide and launching myself into space with the hopes of landing upright."

Alvan had let his wife and Rostov off at the front door and they were making their slow way into the lobby, nodding to the assembled guests.

"Did you have a good day?" Martha asked.

"Yes, wonderful. But they booted us out early. Between the snow and fog on the mountain, visibility is zero and they didn't want to have someone get lost up there. It's so much clearer down here."

The phone rang and Eunice let Brendan know it was for him. It was Daniels, who had wanted to interview the Dalrymples but had other pressing business and asked if Brendan could do the honors. He agreed and arranged to talk to them in the library after they had a chance to freshen up and for him to get out of his ski gear into casual clothes. What he preferred to be doing was getting a hot bath and having a hot toddy, but duty came first.

Martha was first down into the library and had a surprised look on her face as she sat clutching her handbag in her lap.

"Mrs. Dalrymple, this won't be as intimidating as you might imagine."

"I've never talked to the police before. I mean, in such a situation, although obviously I have had conversations with policemen in the past." She blushed a bit at her ramble and covered it with a small smile.

"When did you and your husband get here?"

"The same day you arrived, early in the afternoon. We drove from Albany. Troy, actually. It's not that far." She pushed her glasses back up her nose as they had slid down.

"How long are you going to stay?"

"We thought a few days before going back. A little Christmas present to each other after a long semester." She smiled, displaying her prominent front teeth.

"Your husband teaches. Do you as well?"

"Not really, I serve more as a housemother, making sure the girls are well and have everything they need. Comforting some of those who are homesick."

"I imagine there is a lot of that with the younger ones."

"Yes. And those that have to stay over the summer term. At least they get to play tennis and enjoy the outdoors. Those who stay over the holidays are a bit sad. Oh! I completely forgot! I meant to get some little presents when we were in town but got caught up in other things."

"I suppose you could do that tomorrow if the weather clears up a bit," Brendan said.

"It wasn't too bad driving back out here."

"Well, let's talk about the porter for a bit. Did you speak to him at all?"

"No. He brought the bags up, received a gratuity from Alvan and nodded. Didn't say a word. Even when he waited on our table that evening, he didn't say anything. He came up to the table with a look of expectation, which we took was his shy way of wanting to know our order without actually using those words. Strange behavior from a waiter," she added.

"I think he might have been hired to be a porter first although he had served as a waiter previously in some places."

"Curious."

"Is there anything else you can tell me about him. Anything you noticed?"

"I certainly noticed that Mrs. Browne practically jumped out of her chair when he approached. I thought that was odd."

"Maybe she was startled," Brendan said.

She cocked her head to one side and looked at him with raised eyebrows. Clearly, she did not think that was the explanation.

"Is there something you want to add?"

"Just between you and me, I think she is more than a little strange. Seems to see bogeymen everywhere. That's just my opinion."

Brendan didn't disagree with the observation, he just wondered why this woman felt the need to share it with him. He scribbled some notes as he thought and then said,

"If you think of anything that might be of use, please let me know. And could you ask your husband to come in?"

The Professor came in and sat down, looking a bit rumpled under his tweed jacket. As Brendan glanced at the man's appearance, he smoothed down the front of his sweater and sat forward, giving his full attention to the detective.

"I understand you teach at Emma Willard," Brendan began.

"Yes, history. I love it—ancient Greece and Rome—all the way up to modern times. I'm sorry to say that it might be one girl in thirty who has the remotest interest in the topic. Not that they don't perform well on tests, they simply look bored. Maybe it's this generation."

"I had a history teacher in elementary school who had us dress as Roman centurions. With tin foil or colanders on our heads and old brushes on top to look like helmets and cardboard swords we had the best time. And obviously a memorable one."

"The school wouldn't go in for that sort of fol-de-rol and, frankly, neither would I."

That stopped the conversation for a moment. But Brendan plunged on. "Back to the incident of yesterday, remind me where you and your wife were."

"Oh, yes. The unfortunate Tony."

For a moment, Brendan couldn't remember if they had shared his name with the guests, but let it pass.

"Martha and I wanted to see some of the countryside, bleak as it might be at this time of year, but also some of the historic sites. My wife wanted to see Edith Wharton's house, but I never liked her work. The house, however, what you can see, is spectacular. I was interested in finding a Shaker village that is still in operation here, although I was warned that they didn't appreciate people coming around to stare at them like monkeys in a zoo."

"How long were you gone?"

"Several hours, since we stopped to have a bite to eat."

"Where? I thought it might be hard to find a place open in the middle of December."

Dalrymple laughed. "I can't remember the name of the place and that's probably a good thing! It was just the enclosed porch of someone's home, if you can believe it. They served us soup and sandwiches. It was not bad but hardly a culinary experience I relished. I suppose it's how they make a little money in the cold weather. After we ate, we pottered around more, trying not to get lost or turned around before we headed back here."

"Is there anything else you can tell me about the porter?"

"Nothing at all except our shock at hearing what had occurred."

Brendan felt they had reached the end of any productive information and, looking up, he saw over Dalrymple's shoulder that Amanda was standing in the hallway.

"Thank you very much, sir," Brendan said, standing up and shaking the man's hand. He left, nodding to Amanda as he went out into the hall.

"We're still some time away from dinner. Did you want to interview anyone else?"

"I really haven't talked to Greg or his wife yet. Also, Olive."

"How did this last one go?"

"Totally inconclusive."

"There's something off about him. I've never met an academic who doesn't have an ink stain on his fingers," Amanda said.

Chapter 14

Greg Foster had a peeved look on his face when he entered the library and stood in the doorway. "I've got a business to run, you know."

"I'm well aware, but the sooner we get to the bottom of this, the better. Please sit down."

It was done begrudgingly.

"How did you come about hiring Tony?" Brendan began.

"He just showed up one day, looking for work. Said he had worked as a bellboy and a waiter in several places, gave the names, places I recognized, and that he was traveling south and was robbed the last place he stayed. So, he needed a job and some money to get moving on again."

"He told you up front he wouldn't be here long? And you still hired him?"

"Sure. First snowfall had happened, which meant the ski season would kick into gear. In between winter and spring there's a bit of a lull and when we do repairs and other maintenance. I figured he could help with that, too. And my father was experiencing some health problems, which meant I had to carry the whole load here. Olive is a local girl who boards here when we're busy and goes home during down times. She doesn't mind that it's not full time, which suits us fine."

"How was he as a worker?"

"Good. Strong guy. Didn't hesitate to do whatever I needed him to do. We had to bring in the lawn furniture, take down the tennis nets, store the umbrellas, put traps in the outbuildings. We get mice and rats that like to chew on whatever they can."

"He spoke with an accent?" Brendan asked.

"You tell me. He spoke to you, didn't he?"

"Yes, but murmuring a few words, that's all. There's no way I could place it. Did you think he was from outside the country?"

Greg shrugged and it wasn't until then that Brendan wondered about Greg protecting himself from having hired someone without papers. Not that it wasn't done all the time.

"Hey, I'm not federal enforcement here. I'm trying to get to the bottom of who killed that man, and where he was from could be a significant clue."

"It's a clue I don't have the answer to," Greg said with a tight smile. He looked at his wristwatch.

"I know you've got a meal to get ready, but I imagine Jimmy has that under control. Tell me about buying this place back from Cash Ridley. Your idea or your father's?"

"Cash got bored being up here when his business was in New York. I think he got out of it what he wanted, and it was time to pick up sticks."

"What did he want?"

Greg chuckled. "He liked to invite all his big shot friends and show off his hospitality by giving them free meals and drinks. It took him a while to realize that his pals were more than happy to get a free ride and that the purpose of the hotel business is to make money. And he wasn't. He sold it to us for a very nice price. Couldn't wait to get it off his books."

"Were you pleased to get it back?"

There was a long pause. "Sure. I had other ideas of what we should have done with the money we got from the sale, but Pop was being his cautious self and wanted to wait. And while we waited, the place came back into our orbit. At that price, at that time, we jumped on it. But it hasn't been easy with my father not being able to do as much."

"May I ask, you mentioned health problems?"

"Yes, his heart. He's supposed to take it easy physically and not get too excited. I'm hoping we can get past this whole thing soon. I know he worries about it and the reputation of the hotel."

"Is that something you argue about?" Brendan asked.

"Who says we argue?"

"Loud voices are heard from the office and the kitchen from time to time."

"Who told you that?" Greg leaned forward in the armchair.

"To be honest, I heard what sounded like an argument the first night we were here. If it wasn't you and your father, was it you and Tony?"

"No, it was probably me and Jimmy. He's sometimes wants to get too fancy with the food, and I don't think the guests appreciate it enough."

Brendan didn't buy that explanation and only reacted with raised brows.

"It's true!"

"Your father mentioned something about Tony flirting with your wife and that he yelled at him about it."

"What? No, that doesn't make any sense. Why would my father do that?"

"To protect you?" Brendan asked.

That stopped Greg short. "You don't think my father killed Tony, do you?"

Brendan said nothing.

"He couldn't. He doesn't have the energy to go sneaking around in the guests' rooms looking for a gun—not even knowing someone had a gun—and then stashing it until the next day when Tony would be by himself."

"He very well might not have. But I think you have just described what happened. Except the person who shot Tony knew that Mrs. Browne had a gun and managed to take it and saved it to do the deed later."

Brendan could almost hear the gears in Greg's head moving as he considered all the people who were in the hotel and who could have done it because he was going through the same exercise and still hadn't come up with an easy answer.

"Thank you. Could you ask your wife to come in?"

Greg was still stunned by the thoughts that were racing through his mind and he went out into the hall where he saw his wife stood clearly able to have heard the conversation in the library.

"What are you doing?" he whispered to her.

"Maybe saving your bacon."

He pulled her back toward the entrance to the lobby before saying in a normal tone of voice, "Detective Halloran would like to see you now." He made sure several people in the lobby overheard him before returning to the office behind the lobby desk.

His father was seated at the oak desk in the room, going through receipts and tallying them in an accounting book. George looked up as he heard Greg approach, his son's face like thunder. Greg closed the door.

"What's this I hear about you yelling at Tony?"

"What are you talking about?"

"That cop has got it in his head that you got angry with Tony and killed him."

"He said that?"

Greg sat down and exhaled. "Not exactly. But he suspects us."

"Us? Or me? Or you? You're the hothead."

"You're the one running this place down."

The conversation that had begun in angry whispers soon escalated to loud voices and the two Foster men were unaware that the volume of their argument, if not the content, could be easily heard by the guests in the lobby.

Jimmy came in from the kitchen and propelled his large frame around the lobby desk and pushed through to the office. He slammed the door behind him.

"You two have got to stop. Everyone on this floor can hear you."

The intervention worked and the Fosters calmed down without looking at each other.

"The last thing you want is for that cop to think you're the type of folks to fly off the handle." He glared at them for a few moments more and opened the door and addressed the guests in the lobby.

"As they always say, 'Nothing to see here, folks.'"

His crude attempt at humor got a few chuckles from the group and he went back to the kitchen.

"As if things weren't tense enough here, we've got to listen to the owners squabbling," Caroline said.

"This could very well ruin the business for them," Aggie said, sipping her hot chocolate.

"That would be a shame. This place brings a lot of people to the area," John said. "Maybe I'll talk to Homer at the **Berkshire Eagle** about running a factual article about the death."

"Rather than call it a murder? Which it seems to have been," Louisa said.

"We don't know that yet," Caroline said, and everyone looked at her in astonishment.

"You certainly don't think he shot himself in the chest and then threw the gun across the room."

"That's not what I'm saying! Just don't jump to conclusions!" she said and quickly left the room.

"I'd be worried, too, if it were my mother's gun that was used," Louisa said.

Brendan and Eunice had just begun their conversation when all the shouting had started from the other end of the hallway.

Eunice smiled weakly. "Those two! At it hammer and tongs." She pulled at the back of her short hair behind her ear.

"Do they argue a lot?" Brendan asked.

"For one thing, they're loud people and they're with each other day and night. Despite you folks being here, winter is a tough season for us because it's so dependent on the ski resort having enough snow to be open."

"How did you come to live here?" he asked.

"I'm not from around here. I'm from Springfield. When I finished with high school, I was looking for a job. Work was hard to get there, unless you wanted to work in a factory, which I did not. I saw an ad in the paper for waitresses needed at a 'beautiful scenic resort,' and I thought it would be a nice break to be in the cool mountains for a change. I called and took a bus up here for an interview. That was when Mr. Ridley still owned the place, and I got the feeling he thought it was more important to have attractive waitresses than somebody with experience. I met Greg when the Fosters took it back and, well…"

"The rest is history?" Brendan added to finish her thought.

"When we got married, I thought I would be working the front desk, and I did during the summer. When it's the slow season, it's all hands on deck, as you've seen. So, I'm back to waitress duty for now and some light housekeeping. Olive does more of the heavy-duty work."

"It seems all of you are working from dawn into the late evening."

"Yes. And with so few of us, we still have to have someone available to answer the phone or deal with whatever comes up from the guests. It's so much easier in the summer."

Brendan said, "It must also be much more exciting in the summer with the influx of guests, a band staying and the ballroom open for dancing."

"Oh, yes. And I get to supervise the wait staff, which I enjoy."

"Winter must be isolating," he said.

Eunice's eyes began to fill up. "You can't know what it's like to be stuck here day and night, sometimes with nothing to do if there are no guests. Greg and his father at each other's throats worrying about the lack of guests. Arguments between the staff."

"Which staff?"

"Jimmy and Tony sometimes. Olive and Tony. Olive and Jimmy."

"That's quite a lot of Olive," Brendan said.

"Jimmy teased her because I think she had a crush on Tony."

"And did he reciprocate?"

"Tony was always polite. I overheard that you thought he wasn't American because of his accent. I don't know where he was from. His accent was very slight, but he was self-conscious about it and tried to talk as little as possible. But I knew he couldn't be American because he had such impeccable manners."

"What did he and Jimmy argue about?"

"Jimmy's a big guy and he liked to stand a little too close to Tony, just to annoy him. He also asked Tony to help lift heavy pots when he could do it himself. He knew that he wouldn't get any back talk about it."

"What about Olive and Jimmy?"

"That was about him saying they were going to get married someday."

"Really?"

"I don't know if he means it or is teasing her. Maybe if he says it enough, she'll come to believe it. She could do worse, in my opinion. Her family has a little farm in Richmond and, as you can imagine, farming in this rocky soil is not easy. She took the job here to get away from her family and taking care of younger brothers and sisters. This place must seem so exciting to her," she said with a smile.

"From what you said, you thought so, too, when you first began."

"Of course. I was younger then. Now I do the same job—and more—and don't get paid for it. Mr. Ridley ran the place with champagne flowing, important guests from New York, show people even. There was a band almost every night during the summer. It was grand."

"I get the impression that Mr. Ridley took it on as a hobby and a way to show off to his colleagues and friends."

"And he could afford it. He's a millionaire, for heaven's sake. If he lost money on it, so be it."

"Did Jimmy tease you about Tony?"

Eunice stiffened her back and glared at him. "Of course not. Why would he? Jimmy didn't dare tease me about anything. I'm the owner's daughter-in-law. He wouldn't try it."

She crossed her arms across her chest and continued to give him a stern look.

"One other thing, who has keys to the guest rooms?"

"Obviously they do. And we have a set hanging behind the front desk. Another in the safe in the event a guest checks out and takes it with them."

"If the front desk isn't staffed, anyone could take a key to one of the rooms?"

"I suppose. But it would look strange for someone to be rummaging around behind the front desk."

"I agree. But it's winter, not many staff about, you can't keep the front desk manned twenty-four hours a day. Anybody could have swiped a key if they wanted."

"I suppose. But why? What has this got to do with Tony?"

"Somebody sneaked into Mrs. Browne's room and took her gun. That's what."

Chapter 15

After Eunice left, Brendan got up to stretch his legs by walking down the hallway toward the deserted patio. As he passed by, he noticed how the cold seeped through the floor-to-ceiling windows. The view was of the abandoned tennis courts, the forest stretching behind with fir trees ascending the mountain.

"Bren?" Amanda called from the entrance to the hallway and he turned. "How's it going?"

"All I can say is it's going. It seems like a typical family-run operation with all the good and bad that goes along with it. Petty jealousies, with small issues blown out of proportion."

She walked up, slipped her arm through his and rested her head on his shoulder. "Probably very much out of proportion."

They stood for a few moments watching the snow come down before Brendan said, "Isn't it strange that this should occur at a family-owned hotel with a group of guests who don't really have any connection to one another?"

"Three groups I would say. There are our three couples, the Professor and his wife, Hextilda and Caroline. And I don't know how Rostov fits in. Are these groups connected in some way? Without jumping ahead to a conclusion, it would seem that only the residents of the hotel—the family and staff—had any significant contact with the porter."

"Therefore, it must be one of them?" Brendan asked. "For my sake and the Sheriff's, we have to be as thorough as possible. Someone had it out for Tony, but why? That's what I still can't figure out."

They stood a few more minutes before Brendan bent to kiss Amanda on the top of her head. "I've one last initial interview to go."

"Initial?"

"I think this is going to take a lot longer than we imagined. But first, I've got Olive on my list."

They walked back to the lobby and after Brendan asked Greg where Olive might be, he disappeared down the hall to the kitchen and came back with the young woman. He realized he hadn't paid particular attention to her as she waited on tables in the dining room, but it wasn't because she didn't merit it. She had that certain swagger as she walked beside him, telegraphing that she might not be from the big city, but she was no fool.

After they sat, Brendan began, "I'm glad to finally talk to you."

She stiffened a bit before smiling, which brought her face to life. "Thank you."

"It's awful to have this horrible business lingering. The Sheriff and I really want to get to the bottom of it."

She said nothing, just stared at him with sparkling eyes.

"First, how long have you been working here?"

"Two years. I started as a summer worker and then stayed on as needed because I don't live too far away."

"So, you drive back and forth from home?"

"No, I don't have a car of my own," she said with a small laugh as if that were a ridiculous notion. "I live here most of the time and if they're going through a slow period and don't need me, my father comes and takes me home. My family lives in Richmond."

"That's what Eunice told me."

"I'm not surprised," she said.

"Why do you say that?" Brendan asked, although by her tone he could imagine the answer.

"She's from Springfield. The big city. Never ceases to remind me of it. I've been to Springfield. It's got a lot of smelly factories and a river. That's about it."

"Do you get along?" he asked, feeling as though he was picking at a scab.

"Let's just say we work together. She thinks she can pull the easier jobs because she's the boss's daughter-in-law. In the summer, she's at the front desk as smug as can be while the rest of us gals are doing up the rooms. She pretends she's still working for Mr. Ridley, who encouraged her to smile and flirt with the customers with that phony laugh." She gave a rendition of a feminine laugh starting out on a high note and ending mid-tone. "At least I don't have to listen to it all day like her husband. It drives Greg nuts." She realized she may have said too much and was quiet.

"How did Eunice get along with Jimmy and Tony?"

"She thinks she's the boss of Jimmy and she's not. He just lets it roll off his back. That's his way. She thought she was the boss of Tony, too. He put up with it, but he was planning on leaving anyway. Just saving up enough to go south."

"I imagine there are more staff in the summer."

"Gosh, yes. Waiters, busboys, another cook, porters, maids. The place is buzzing in the summer, it's so busy."

"It seems when there are fewer guests in the winter, you all are thrown together more."

"I'll say. Cabin fever, they call it." She gave a short laugh. "Eunice may look down her nose at me, but I get paid. And I'm saving it up."

"What are you planning on doing with it?"

"I call it my Running Away From Home money. Not running exactly, but I might go to some new place and work there. Get away from here." She looked at him and turned on a smile. "You wouldn't happen to have a cigarette, would you?"

"I'm sorry, I don't smoke."

"Oh."

"Where was Tony planning on going?"

"He just said south. I don't know."

"New York? Or farther south like Florida?"

"I said I don't know."

"Mexico?"

Olive put her lips together in a line but said nothing.

"Were you by any chance thinking of going with him?"

"He mentioned it to me, but, of course, I didn't take him seriously. I thought he was teasing me. He said the same thing to Eunice when we were all in the kitchen and Jimmy jumped right in and volunteered to go, too. It was just a joke."

Brendan looked down at the small notebook where he had written some words and could see that she was trying to figure out what they were. Eunice appeared in the doorway.

"There you are. We need to get ready for dinner," she said and left.

"Yes, ma'am," Olive muttered. "I guess we're done here," she said as she got up.

"For now. Thank you."

Between Brendan and the Sheriff, they had interviewed everyone who was either a worker at the hotel or a guest, and he still didn't have any clearer notion of what had transpired. He decided to call Daniels and discuss it with him. He went to the front desk and, seeing George in the office behind, asked if he could use the telephone.

"Sure, sure."

"It's a private call, if you don't mind."

"As long as it's not long distance," George chuckled, knowing full well who Brendan would be calling.

After the door closed, Brendan asked the operator to connect him. He wondered if she would be listening in on the conversation as most operators in small towns did, so his first question to Daniels was, "Is it safe to talk on the phone here?"

The Sheriff laughed. "If you mean is the operator listening in, she very well might be. But it's my wife's shift, so she already knows more about everything than I do. How's it going?"

"Very slowly. Each of the staff has some issue with another. It may be because they are cooped up here in the winter having to do all the tasks. It didn't help that they got slammed with taking care of the six of us as well as the other five guests. That's a lot of people to mix drinks for, feed and deliver hot cocoa up to the rooms in the middle of the night." Brendan looked at his wristwatch. "I was going to call the Emma Willard School to verify that the Professor is who he says he is, but it's too late now. Tomorrow. Are you coming back here then?"

"I've got some stuff going on here. Someone passed a counterfeit bill, if you can imagine."

"Big city crime comes to the country. At least I think I picked up a smidgen of information from Olive. She said that Tony told them he was saving up to go to south although they thought he was teasing since he invited Eunice and Olive to go with him."

"It sounds like it could have been his intent based on his comings and goings from his passport."

"My question is whether he was telling the truth," Brendan said.

"About taking one of the women with him or leaving the country?"

Brendan chuckled. "One thing I know, we're not any closer to figuring it out."

"We could always blame an unknown assailant—and by definition, that's what we have so far. I'll be popping around in the morning to chew things over with you. Maybe something will register in my brain by then."

DINNER THAT EVENING had a strange and contrasting tone. The wait staff, Eunice and Olive, each suspicious that the other had spoken about her with Brendan, were sullen and keeping their distance. The large table with three couples and Caroline were conscious of the tension in the room but struggled to keep up a lively conversation. By contrast, Mrs. Browne, Rostov and the Dalrymples were in good humor as they enjoyed a bottle of wine together.

"I don't suppose you've gotten any closer to solving this," Caroline said.

Brendan looked up, startled out of whatever thoughts were circling in his brain. "Of course, I can't comment," he said.

"I talked to José while you were getting ready for dinner."

"How is he?" Louisa asked.

"I'm sure the Oasis is chugging along," Rob said.

"He's fine, the Oasis is packed, and Boston is cold and overcast."

"Hardly a surprise," Louisa said.

"The department store windows are in full holiday display."

"Oh," Aggie said. "I wish I could see that. I used to love walking past the stores in Manhattan at this time of year. Always some new design with motorized elves and, of course, the model trains."

"We can pop over to Boston at least for a day next weekend," John suggested.

"Please do. Come stay with us and we'll make a night of it. Out on the town, window shopping…"Amanda said.

"Or actual shopping," Louisa said. "Wink, wink."

"The important news is more unsettling, and I haven't told Mother yet. I don't want to break up the mood of that jolly foursome who act as though nothing has happened. It seems that José discovered who sent a kidnap note to my mother."

"So, it was a note? I thought you were uncertain about that."

"I was. Mother went into one of her vague moods and wouldn't tell me the specifics. But it was a note, and she shared it with my husband. And it turns out the culprit was not some political group or sinister cabal. It was Bannister."

The other six people at the table said in unison, "Who?"

"The new man that she hired only last month. He wasn't aware that Mother and I had left town and was busy constructing another note demanding a large sum of money when one of the maids came upon him. She, of course, told José and the jig was up, as they say."

"I don't think I've ever said that, but if that's all it was about, I'm glad to hear it," Brendan said.

"Therefore, neither my mother nor I had any reason to be here in the first place. Nor did either of us have a reason to shoot the porter," Caroline said, smiling over her wine glass in triumph.

"With the information you now have, that's true. But you didn't have it before. If you had, you wouldn't have come here with your mother," Brendan said.

"And if you had stayed in Boston, you might have been kidnapped by that Bannerman fellow," Amanda added.

"Bannister. Like on a staircase," Caroline corrected. After another moment she asked, "So my mother and I are still suspects?"

"I wouldn't use that term exactly," Brendan said. "But the Sheriff will be here tomorrow, and we'll see if we can put the pieces of the puzzle together."

Caroline put her glass down abruptly and left the table.

"Oops," Amanda said.

"Thanks, Brendan. I think you just lost me a customer," Louisa said, thinking of the dresses she had designed with Caroline in mind that now might not be purchased.

"You don't think she'll shun you or Monsieur Josef because of this, do you?" Amanda asked.

"You might not know her as well as I do," Rob said. "She can really hold a grudge."

"And I'm sure I don't have to remind you to make sure your doors are locked tonight," Brendan reminded them.

Chapter 16

As they were getting into pajamas for the night, Louisa said to her sister, "I was upset and sorry about the death of the porter, of course. But suddenly, with nothing resolved, I'm scared."

"I imagine whoever did that to him has no reason to harm us."

Louisa stared at her. "I know it wasn't one of our group—we have no connection to this place at all. Except Aggie and John but that's beyond belief that they would be involved. I think it must be one of the staff, but who? And why?"

"Brendan told me that there were some petty jealousies among the staff, especially Eunice and Olive. But to steal a gun and shoot someone?"

"How could any of the staff have done that? They were all in town, remember?"

"That doesn't mean someone couldn't have doubled back at some point," Amanda said. "George and Greg had access to a car and any one of the others could have hitched a ride back."

"Wouldn't someone have spoken up about that by now? Not the staff, but a member of the public?"

"Aggie mentioned to me after she first moved here that she was surprised at how insular these small communities can be. Even in times of trouble, they are reluctant to give up one of their own."

"Even in the case of murder?" Louisa asked.

"Memories are long, and families live here for generations. It's not like the big city where you can just move to another neighborhood and hope your past doesn't catch up with you. Or the fact that you ratted someone out will be forgotten."

"It's so funny to hear you talk like that, Amanda. Mother would have a fit if she were here."

"I would have sent her packing the instant we learned of the death of that poor man. And unless there is some reason for Brendan to stay, I think we might look to get out of here tomorrow."

THE MOUNTAIN AIRE had its creaks and groans in the night when all else was quiet, but snuggled under wool blankets with the door locked, the sisters slept comfortably for several hours. Sometime in the early hours, Amanda became restless, bothered by the scratchy blanket under her chin and repositioning the sheet to prevent further contact, turned herself over. Her eyes popped open as she thought she heard someone walking down the hall. She sat up and cocked her head to hear a slight rattle. Then silence and again footsteps. As they got closer, her heart started to pound so that she couldn't be sure whether she was hearing her fear or an actual sound.

The footsteps stopped outside her door, and she could hear and just about see in the semi-darkness of faint moonlight, the doorknob turn back and forth. Amanda realized he or she was testing for an unlocked door. And no, she realized, it was not Brendan checking that everyone was safe in their beds. He wouldn't do that. Whoever it was, the sound of footfalls as they made their way down the hall became fainter. Her mind reeled between wanting to put her head under the covers and forget about it and pulling the door open to see what was out there.

Ignoring the chilly room and not pausing to put on a robe or slippers, she tiptoed to the door and put her ear against it. The sounds became fainter, and she realized the person had moved down the corridor and had not gained entry to any of the rooms. What about the staff who slept in the floor above? Were they safe? Against her better judgment, she quietly unlocked the door and ever so slowly pulled it open. She didn't have the courage yet to step out into the hall, just enough to listen intently to the footsteps moving away. She couldn't tell if it was a man or a woman, and as curiosity got the better of her, she put her head out and inched her torso forward to see if she could ascertain who or what was lurking in the hall. Faint moonlight shone through the window at one end of the hall and she thought she made out a figure flattened against the opposite wall. Neither she nor the figure moved for long moments.

Was she imagining it, or did the figure seem to slide along the wall almost like some supernatural creature, coming slowly in her direction but on the other side of the hall. Her mouth went dry as she sought to call out or ask who was there before she made the quick decision to go back into her room and lock the door. She turned and in a swift moment someone came up behind her and landed a sharp blow to the back of her head and she slumped to the ground.

Amanda must have cried out, although she didn't remember doing so later, because suddenly doors were unlocked and people streamed into the hall, while someone had the good sense to finally turn on the hall light.

Louisa rushed to the open door, almost stepping on her sister, before making sense of the scene and seeing that Amanda had fallen.

"Was she sleepwalking?" Caroline asked, briskly coming forward.

Louisa had bent down to turn Amanda over and found blood on her own hand. "No, it seems she's been attacked!"

John and Aggie pushed through the throng, and he quickly ascertained that she had indeed been hit on the head. He checked her pulse. Brendan came dashing up, tying his robe into place.

"She's alive," John said.

Louisa gasped and fell backward, never having imagined that her sister would not be alive.

"Let's get her inside."

Louisa turned the light on in the room and dashed to the bathroom to fetch a towel.

John and Brendan picked Amanda up and gently brought her into the bedroom and placed her on the bed, Louisa moving the towel beneath her head. She then started patting Amanda's hand.

"Wake up, please wake up. Should we keep doing this or what?" Louisa asked, unfamiliar with such an event.

"Here, let me," Aggie said, moving Louisa out of the way.

John had already repositioned Amanda, so her airway was unobstructed and then felt gently at the back of her head. "It broke the skin, but the bleeding seems to be minimal."

Amanda groaned and attempted to sit up.

"Not yet, my girl," John said, gently pushing her back down.

"Thank goodness she's so hard-headed," Louisa said, laughing a bit before breaking down in sobs on her own bed. Rob pushed his way into the room, sat with her and patted her on the back.

"What do we do now?" Rob asked.

The hallway was now crowded with all the guests except Rostov who was struggling to open his door and maneuver his crutches.

"What is happening?" he asked.

Olive and Jimmy, the staff who lived on the floor above, had come down after hearing the commotion, but the Fosters' rooms were on the first floor in a wing off the office and they were not present.

"I'll get Mr. Foster," Olive said, her hair in pin curls with a net tied at the base of her neck, taking off at lightning speed to the elevator.

"Please give us a little space," Aggie asked. She went to get another towel from the bathroom, aware that concussion victims often vomited and wanting to give her cousin privacy and breathing room.

"What was she doing in the corridor?" Brendan asked Louisa, his dark hair flopping onto his forehead.

"I have no idea! I woke up when I heard her cry out and tumble against the open door."

"What's going on?" asked Professor Dalrymple from the hallway, his wife trailing behind him and craning her neck to see into the room.

"There's been an accident," John said.

"Amanda must have been sleepwalking and fallen down."

Murmurs of concern were heard and then Brendan took charge and asked everyone to go back to their own rooms. He blew out a gust of air and surveyed the room, which still had five people besides himself. He closed the door.

"I feel sick to my stomach," Amanda said, trying to sit up.

"At least she can talk. Someone needs to stay with her," John said.

"I'm here," Louisa said.

"I mean, someone needs to stay awake while they stay with her. If she sleeps, she needs to be awakened every hour or so to make sure she doesn't lapse into something deeper."

Louisa's eyes widened and she didn't dare ask what the 'something deeper' could be.

"You've heard the nursery rhyme: It's raining, it's pouring, the old man is snoring. He bumped his head and went to bed and didn't get up in the morning," Aggie said.

Louisa was still silent but very pale.

"Do you think you could do that?" he asked.

"I'll do it," Brendan volunteered. "Let me get the book I was reading. Louisa, if you want to stay here to sleep, that's fine. I need to sit upright in the chair, or I will conk out for sure."

"All right," Louisa said.

"A bit unorthodox, but it will be fine," John said.

"How's this. Come stay in my room, Louisa. I'm sure John will want to remain here," Aggie offered her cousin and that seemed to suit everyone better.

"Bren?" Amanda asked.

"What is it?"

"Whoever it was had been trying all the doors to see if they were locked. And whoever it was moved quickly and silently."

They were quiet for a few moments digesting this bit of information before the spell was broken and Rob said good night again. He escorted Aggie and Louisa to the Taylors' room while Brendan left to fetch his book. John had pulled up a chair next to Amanda's bed and smiled at her.

"That was quite a hard knock you got. There will be a nice lump in no time."

"My head is pounding," Amanda said.

"Poor thing," Brendan said when he returned.

"If you brought any aspirin, we could try that. If the pain gets worse, I have some tablets you can take." Following her directions, he went to the bathroom and found her kit, bringing back a glass of water and two pills. "I'm going to stretch out on this other bed. Brendan, I'd say about once an hour make sure to wake her. It's already after two o'clock so not many rounds needed. I'll be alert enough to take over if you can't."

"Aren't you going to sleep?" Brendan asked John.

"I can do the physician's sleep I learned when I was an intern. Fully asleep but able to wake up quickly. Not a good long-term way to gain rest, but efficient for short bursts."

There was a knock on the door.

Brendan opened it to see Olive and George and he stepped out into the hall.

"Did she fall or was she struck?" the owner asked.

"We're putting out the story that she might have been sleepwalking, but she was struck by someone who was lurking in the hall, trying the doors to see if any were unlocked."

"This is very bad. Very bad. Is she all right?"

"John says a concussion. But he's treating it, and she'll have to take it easy for a bit."

"I don't know whether to send all of you away in the

morning or insist that all of you stay until this is sorted out," George said.

"The Sheriff will be here and I'm sure he'll want everyone to stay put for the time being," Brendan said.

Chapter 17

Amanda, Brendan and John made it through a night of interrupted sleep to wake to the sun streaming through the window and snow clouds forming to the north.

"How are you feeling this morning?" John asked Amanda, who had awakened to the bright light.

"I still have a headache, but not as bad as last night. And you're right, I have what feels like a goose egg on the back of my head. Although I've never actually seen or felt a goose's egg." She sat up and winced as she felt under her hair for the spot.

"Let me see," John said, palpating the area gently. He leaned her forward to get a better look at the back of her head. "The blood we saw last night was superficial, but it scared the heck out of Louisa."

Their conversation wakened Brendan who had been asleep in the armchair with his head tilted to the side. He groaned as he straightened up and rubbed his neck. "I think we all need a significant amount of coffee and a good breakfast."

After a few yawns, he pulled himself out of the chair, stretched and looked at Amanda. "You look pretty good after what happened. I didn't want to pepper you with too many questions last night, but do you have any idea who did this to you? A man? A woman? Tall? Short?"

"Easy now," John said. "It's quite common for people with head injuries not to remember what transpired before the event."

"I don't know what woke me up exactly, but I heard footsteps in the hall. Very faint, as if someone were trying not to be detected. And then the doorknob was rattled as if testing to see if it were locked. The hair stood up on the back of my neck."

"I'm sure."

"Then I heard the person continue down the hall, very slowly, stopping periodically as if checking each room. I couldn't stand not knowing who or what was out there, so I opened the door very carefully. I suppose I didn't take into account that the moonlight from the one end of the hall was such that he—or she—could see me, but I still couldn't see much except a figure in the shadows moving quickly. I knew I was in danger and turned to go back into my room. Then bam! Hit on the head."

"Lucky for you that you crashed through the open door, alerting Louisa."

"I feel terrible about the whole thing. Why did I do that? I could have been killed." Amanda's lower lip began to quiver but she turned away from them.

Brendan sat down beside her on the bed and hugged her. "Don't do that again, all right?"

She nodded and blinked away tears.

"Well, I'm all for a shower then breakfast. Brendan, will you stay with her until I get either Aggie or Louisa to take over? I don't think she should be left alone."

"Good idea. Once one of them appears, I'll shower and get food to bring up here. We'll have breakfast in bed," Brendan said with a smile.

Louisa was the first one to relieve Brendan and rushed to her sister to embrace her. "You had us all so worried," she said. "What came over you to confront someone in the dark in the middle of the night?"

"Overconfidence and maybe a touch of stupidity."

"It's too bad you didn't get to grab a fistful of hair or scratch his face. Then we'd know who was creeping about."

"It all happened so fast. I didn't have time to think. You always think you'll be prepared for a situation like that, but when the time comes…"

"I'm going to wash up and get dressed," Louisa said, turning around to lock the door. "Don't let anybody in."

John and Aggie went down to the dining room together and were surprised to find that only the coffee carafes, cups and saucers had been put out. Eunice wheeled a trolley in as they stood by the empty buffet table, her face contorted in a grim frown.

"She's flown the coop!" she said, placing a platter of scrambled eggs on the table with a thump. Then a plate of toast likewise slammed down. She looked up at their inquisitive faces.

"Olive. Olive sneaked off in the night. Left me and Jimmy to put the entire breakfast together."

"How did she leave? Surely, she didn't walk out in the dark?" John asked.

"She must have called her father or brother to pick her up. When I went upstairs to see what was keeping her a while ago, her stuff was gone. Not that she kept a lot here, but she did a flit for sure. And now I'm stuck doing everything. I may just call a friend in town and take off myself."

She gave them one last furious look and wheeled the trolley out of the room.

Brendan nearly collided with her as he entered the dining room.

"What's that fury all about?"

"Olive left," John said.

Brendan sighed and shook his head. "Is she sure Olive left of her own volition?"

"I don't think the mystery prowler took her away after packing her things for her," Aggie said.

"The Sheriff will be here soon. I'm taking breakfast up to Amanda and once I've had several cups of coffee, I'll fill him in on the entire situation. It could be that her family came to take her out of danger and, if so, the Sheriff knows where they live."

He took two plates and piled them high with eggs and toast, there being no bacon or sausages yet, stuffed silverware in his pockets and made his way to the elevator. After leaving the food in Amanda's room, he came back down, appropriated two cups and one of the coffee carafes and went back upstairs. It was then that he told Amanda and Louisa about Olive's quick disappearance.

"I don't blame her," Louisa said. "If I were her, I would have gone right after the poor porter was killed."

"Maybe all of us should have done the same," Amanda said. "Louisa, why don't you get some breakfast yourself. And keep your eyes and ears open."

"Can't I just have a meal with no drama?" She flounced out of the room.

"She provides her own drama," Amanda said, biting into some toast. "Gosh, I'm awfully hungry for some reason."

They had only a few minutes to themselves before there was a knock on the door.

"Sorry," said Caroline, peeping around the door that Brendan had partially opened. "I was wondering how Amanda was doing." He let her in.

"You look very good, actually. I'm surprised. Maybe it wasn't such a bad bump after all."

She reached onto the platter with the toast, took a slice and sat on the other bed. "You don't mind, do you?"

"Go right ahead," said Amanda after the fact.

Caroline took a bite, chewed it and looked at Brendan. "Amanda, I wanted to talk to you about something." She looked back at Brendan. "In confidence, if you don't mind." She put on her prettiest smile.

"I'll just step outside," he said, annoyed.

After the door had closed, Caroline leaned in toward

Amanda and said in a loud whisper, "I'm worried about my mother."

"In what respect?" Amanda said, thinking there were many reasons to be worried.

"She had her things on the bed and then went into the bathroom. I noticed her handbag looked lumpy again and I feared she had somehow got hold of another gun. Not that she had anything to do with the shooting of the porter, of course. She may have already bought another gun when she was in town with the Dalrymples, not knowing at the time that the kidnap issue was moot. Anyway, I opened her handbag and saw a huge pile of bills."

"I don't understand."

"Money. Cash. Fifties and hundreds. It must have been thousands of dollars."

"What? What is your mother doing with that out here, much less anywhere?"

"I don't know. I didn't have the nerve to ask her, so I just let it ride until after she and I have breakfast and then I'm going to confront her. I just needed to tell someone and with your professional interest in such things, perhaps you had a suggestion of what I should do."

"Absolutely ask her. And as soon as possible."

Caroline got up and paced the floor in front of Amanda's bed. "I don't know if I can. She can be so irrational."

"What are you afraid of? That she will put you and José out of the house?"

Caroline bit her thumb. "Frankly, yes. In spite of her thinking it's not a problem for her to bring that Rostov fellow in as a permanent guest, she has been dropping hints about how crowded the house will be once Valerie moves in after she and Fred are married."

"They'll be sharing a room, I assume, so what's the problem? It's only one more mouth to feed."

Caroline continued her pacing. "It's more than that. My mother doesn't particularly like Valerie."

"Oh dear. She's so inoffensive, how could that be?"

"That's just the problem. She wishes Valerie would have more of an opinion on things. Not be so wishy-washy."

Amanda laughed. "Does she want a daughter-in-law to verbally spar with her? That could get old very fast."

"I think it's because of her lack of assertion that my mother doesn't respect her. You know how she barrels over anyone who won't stand up to her. I also think she is afraid that Valerie is going to ingratiate herself to the point of making my mother feel that she is being followed all the time by a puppy. She'll hate being at home. Although that might not be so bad from my perspective."

By this time Caroline had worked her way over to the window and surveyed the sky. "Looks like more snow coming today." Then her eyes were drawn down to the front of the hotel where a car had pulled up. "I think the Sheriff is back," she said. "No, wait! That's my mother getting in the car. That's the Dalrymples' car! Where is she going now?"

Caroline ran out of the room, almost crashing into Brendan, who was waiting outside.

"What's going on?" he asked Amanda.

"Mrs. Browne is on the move again with her new best friends."

"I specifically asked them not to leave until the Sheriff got here. That blasted woman!"

He went over to the window to see the car driving away. "Caroline will never catch up with her."

A key turned in the lock and Louisa came in.

"I thought we only had one key between us?" Amanda asked.

"Yes, but I thought you might be sleeping, so I asked Greg to give me another key."

"That he pulled from behind the front desk," Brendan said.

"Yes."

"That seems to eliminate some people from being the middle-of-the-night prowler," he said.

"How so?" Louisa asked.

"If it were George, Greg or Eunice, Olive or Jimmy, they could get into any of the rooms with the help of that extra set of keys. So, it must have been someone who didn't know where the duplicates were stored."

"That only leaves one of our party. Which is ridiculous," Amanda said. "Isn't it?"

"Or Caroline. Or Hextilda," Louisa said.

"Or the Dalrymples," Brendan said.

"I'm so frustrated that I can't pull any clue out of my memory that would help identify who that was last night.

I'd like to suggest it was a man from the force of the blow. But a woman with the element of surprise and a strong arm could have inflicted the same damage."

Louisa sat on the other bed and Brendan leaned against the dresser.

"Let's look at this logically. It could have been the owners or the staff who were trying the doors. If they used a key, they would obviously put themselves under suspicion," Brendan said.

"Back to the murder for a moment. Remember that someone said the staff had just been paid, yet Tony had no money in his pockets. Who would know there was money to be found except the owners or one of the staff who had just got paid themselves," Amanda said.

"It could have been a random stranger who tried to make it look like a robbery," Louisa suggested.

"Yes, but Mrs. Browne's gun was used. Whoever used it took it either the first night we were here or the next morning while she was at breakfast. No one could have entered the building, gone up to her room and stolen a gun; they would have had to know there was one to begin with!" Amanda said.

"If Hextilda didn't lock her room when she went to breakfast that morning and left her handbag in the room, anyone could have taken it. Anyone who overheard the conversation in the dining room the night before," Brendan said. "Any one of the diners or staff."

"Caroline had the easiest access to it," Amanda said.

"And the notion that someone stole her gun was just her word for it. Yes, I'm afraid it may come back to Caroline or

Mrs. Browne, who thought Tony was part of the kidnap scheme, and, thinking all the staff were gone, was frightened to see that he was still in the building."

"But Caroline was skiing with us, remember?" Louisa said.

"She came back early. She told everyone that. Remember, she was the one who told our entire table at dinner the night before, in full earshot of the other guests and the staff, that her mother had a gun. What if she were setting us all up as possible suspects? And then eliminating herself by saying she didn't know how to shoot a gun?"

They pondered the possibilities under Brendan said, "Louisa, if you stay here with your sister, I'll go down and wait for the Sheriff."

"Oh, no, you don't," Amanda said, getting out of bed. "I am not going to stay in bed or in this room with a chaperone while you do all the exciting stuff." She walked to the bathroom. "I'm going to get washed up and dressed, if you don't mind, Detective Halloran."

Brendan and Louisa followed her to the bathroom door,

"I don't think this is advisable," he said. "You probably need to be cleared by John first."

"Amanda, you are always the logical one. Be reasonable and stay inside in case whoever it is comes back."

She stopped at the entrance to the bathroom. "I feel like a sitting duck here in the room when everyone knows where I am. While you all go about your day, I'll be a perfect target. No, I'm going to wash up, fix my hair, do my makeup and get dressed. Amanda Burnside is on the job again."

Chapter 18

Amanda was still a little wobbly, but she wasn't about to let Brendan know. A believer in the power of positive thinking, she put on her favorite lipstick, a brave face, pulled her shoulders back and she was ready.

"Just don't overdo things," Brendan said, tucking her arm in his. "You know John and Aggie won't like this at all."

"Our first order of action is to avoid them at all costs. I'm armed with a good dose of aspirin and another of resolve. That will get me through the morning at least."

They came down to the lobby to see that the Sheriff had arrived and was in conversation with Eunice and Greg, who showed more interest in the missing Olive than they had when she worked there.

"Did either of you or your father hear a car pull up during the early-morning hours?" Daniels asked them.

"After all the business with the supposed prowler," Eunice

began and, then turning, saw Amanda approaching and stopped speaking.

"Go on," Amanda said.

"With all the business earlier, we were extremely tired and I, for one, slept soundly."

"If a car came into the drive, they had their headlights off, because we can usually see them even through the thick curtains."

"Sounds very inconvenient for you," the Sheriff remarked.

"On the one hand, yes, it can disturb your sleep. On the other, we know when someone is approaching to inquire about a room after regular work hours. That and the bell at the front desk. We don't like to turn down potential guests."

"So, you didn't have anyone on the front desk?"

"Of course not. Not with so few guests. We keep the front door unlocked in the event someone is lost in a storm. Money is locked in the safe and we assume our guests lock themselves in their rooms. We wouldn't like to deny someone in dire need. Of course, in the summer season we have someone on the desk all twenty-four hours because we have so many people coming and going. You can't imagine the requests we get in the middle of the night."

Daniels put on an inquisitive look.

"For room service, is what I mean," Greg clarified.

"Back to last night or this morning, you're saying that you didn't hear a car pull up?"

"That's right," Greg said.

"If Olive got nervous about someone prowling, maybe she called her family to take her home. No offense," Daniels said, "but I know her father is a strict man and wasn't too pleased that she was working here. He would rather she stayed on the farm, of course."

"Understood," Greg said. "You can try to call them. They're on a party line, by the way," he said by way of letting the Sheriff know not to reveal too many details during the conversation in the event one of the neighbors might be listening in.

Daniels went into the office behind the front desk and made the call. He came back a few minutes later.

"No, she's not at home. And now we have an irate father and worried mother to deal with."

Eunice grabbed her husband's arm. "You don't think she left and walked somewhere on her own?"

"Carrying a suitcase?" Greg countered. "Somebody came to pick her up. But who? Does she have a boyfriend?" he asked his wife.

"How should I know? She didn't confide in me about anything."

"She's gone and so are the Dalrymples, Mrs. Browne and Mr. Rostov," Brendan said. "The foursome left while we were upstairs."

"What! I asked that nobody leave!" Daniels thundered. "I want to see Olive's room."

All five piled into the elevator to the staff floor.

"This was hers," Eunice pointed at a closed door.

It opened to a small room with a single bed, dresser, chair and desk that seemed to have been used as a vanity by the last resident, based on the mirror propped against the wall above it.

Eunice made a disapproving noise, picked up the mirror and placed it back atop the dresser where it belonged.

"Please, don't touch anything else," the Sheriff said. "In fact, it would be best if you waited in the hall. Detective Halloran?" he summoned. Amanda decided to wait in the hall so as not to aggravate an already tense situation.

There was a small communal area in the middle of the wide hall with a loveseat, two armchairs and a coffee table. Greg, Eunice and Amanda parked themselves there while the other two searched. Eunice made a disapproving noise and shook her head.

"No boyfriend, then?" Amanda asked.

"She flirted like nobody's business, but who knows?"

"Was she involved with Tony, by any chance?"

Eunice looked away and allowed Greg to answer. "Not that I know of. But I wasn't in her company that much. Eunice? What do you say?"

"I'm saying nothing because I can't think of anything nice to say about her at this point."

She crossed her arms over her chest and pressed her lips together.

Daniels and Brendan had searched Olive's room without finding anything more than a stray bobby pin.

"Let's look in the other rooms," the Sheriff said as they were exiting.

"There's Jimmy's room and Tony's, but nobody has been in the other rooms since the season was over," Greg said getting up. "That's Jimmy's," he pointed. "Look, I've got to get back downstairs. Eunice?" he asked, and she got up and followed him to the elevator.

The Sheriff knocked on Jimmy's door out of courtesy even though they had heard him in the kitchen downstairs earlier. It had the same furniture as Olive's room but appeared smaller because there was so much littering the floor. Newspapers, an ashtray with butts, an empty Coke bottle and a pair of shoes were next to the bed. Pajamas, a robe and a towel had been flung onto the unmade bed.

Daniels looked through the drawers of the desk while Brendan moved the clothes on hangers along the pole in the closet.

"Not much here," he said nudging a suitcase with his foot to determine if it was full or empty. The dull thud led him to snap open the latches to find it half-full of clothes. "I wonder if he is planning an escape, too," Brendan said pointing to it.

Daniels came closer. "Maybe. But the drawers are full. Maybe he just ran out of space."

"Do you think he and Olive had something going?" Brendan asked.

"If you're asking me what single people do these days, I'm the wrong man. Been married for twenty-three years. I don't think there's anything here of interest. Let's look into the other rooms, just in case."

Brendan didn't know what the Sheriff expected to find, but he hoped it wasn't a body.

Each room had the same layout with furniture in exactly the same position with a rolled-up mattress on the metal box spring. They looked through each chest of drawers and desk drawer and the empty closets. It was only when they got to a room at the end of the corridor that Brendan put his hand up on the shelf in the closet and felt something soft. He withdrew his hand quickly, fearing it was a dead animal, but then took a hanger from the pole and pushed it onto the floor where it landed with a thud. It was a woman's purse.

"What in the world?" Daniels sputtered.

Brendan opened it carefully. "Money," he said. "Lots of it." He pulled out a stack of bills and whistled.

"Now who do you think wanted to hide this up here? In an unlocked room where anybody could get hold of it?"

Daniels laughed. "Who cares? It's counterfeit!"

Brendan started to laugh and that got Amanda's attention and she went to the room from where the laughter had come.

"Would you like some?" Brendan asked fanning out a handful of bills to her wide-eyed expression. "It's phony."

"I think I'm getting an idea of who passed the bad bill yesterday in town. It was the jolly foursome who had lunch in the café and a man who paid the bill. That means either Dalrymple or Rostov."

"What did I say about Dalrymple?" Amanda added, looking at Brendan.

"It's time to call the school and see if he is who he says he is," Brendan agreed.

"Suppose he really is a professor or teacher?" Amanda asked.

"It doesn't mean that he couldn't be passing counterfeit money. An odd hobby or part-time job, but I've heard of stranger things."

They retreated to the lobby and Brendan asked to use the office telephone. He came back several minutes later. "Not many people at the school because it's holiday break. But there is indeed a Professor Dalrymple who teaches there."

Amanda sighed in frustration.

"Except he is a young Scottish gentleman. And he is not married."

Chapter 19

"But where is my mother?" Caroline asked, overhearing part of the revelation about Dalrymple. "And if he isn't who he says he is, who is he? What do they want with my mother?"

Rob and Louisa had been sitting in the lobby in front of the fireplace and looked at each other.

"Do you think that they meant to kidnap her and not me? And hold her for ransom?"

"Wait a minute," Brendan said, holding up his hands. "You said you learned that the kidnap scheme was something one of your mother's employees was trying to pull off. Why should you think that suddenly these other guests had the same idea, only involving your mother?"

"Because of the money I saw in her handbag this morning. Before she left with the other three. To go who knows where?"

"Are you sure the money was authentic?" Amanda asked.

"How should I know?"

"Was it in her usual handbag or another, smaller one?"

"In that large bag she hauls around." Caroline wrung her hands.

"Why don't you sit down," Brendan suggested. He realized Rob and Louisa were present but since everyone was bound to know what was going on sooner or later, he continued. "This may sound far-fetched, but do you think your mother suspected something about fake bills?"

"If she did, she didn't tell me."

"Is it likely that Mrs. Browne found the illegal money and stashed it up in one of the staff's rooms for safekeeping?" Brendan asked.

"Oh, really, Detective. Who would do such a harebrained thing?" Daniels stopped short as all eyes were now on him.

"You don't know my mother," Caroline said.

He turned to George and asked him if he had the make of car the Dalrymples were driving and the license plate.

"Actually, I do!" he said, scurrying into his office to retrieve the register. "By habit, mostly. In this offseason I normally wouldn't ask, but in the summertime, we have people who come for a drink or a meal and use all the paved parking spaces, leaving none for our guests."

Daniels put the register on the desk and copied out the information.

"Phone, please," he asked George, who was now fully engaged in tracking down the missing guests.

"They better not stiff me on the bill!" he said.

Daniels beckoned to Brendan and they closed the door to the office behind them so those in the lobby could only hear murmuring.

"We've got counterfeit bills, someone pretending to be someone else, four people on a mysterious errand and what does this have to do with the porter?" Amanda asked.

"Clearly he knew something," Rob said.

"What? What was so dire that he needed to be silenced?"

Rob shrugged. "I expect we'll know something soon," he added.

"How can you be so calm at a time like this?" Caroline asked.

He patted her on the shoulder. "Because it doesn't do any good to get excited. Are you sure your mother didn't tell you where she was going or why?"

"Just that there was business to take care of. I don't know what. She's always so vague."

They sat quietly waiting for the office door to open and have some new information. It was twenty minutes later that the two law enforcement officers exited.

"I've called to have the one deputy on duty be on the lookout for the car that has New York license plates. Unfortunately, this close to the state line, that's not so unusual. People from New York sometimes come over to do business. Nobody else has reported getting passed counterfeit bills, but some merchants might not know what to look for."

"The bills in the bag were fifties and one hundreds. That's unusual, don't you think?" Amanda asked.

"They may have got cold feet and tried not to use any more just yet. They'd have a better chance passing them in Boston or New York. Merchants in the big cities might be more aware, but there's a better chance that they could fob off a bit before being caught," Daniels said.

"Wouldn't they be savvy enough to catch it happening?" Amanda asked.

"If it's not a Mom-and-Pop store, there will be more employees, some of them young enough not to know the difference," Brendan said. "Still, those are pretty big bills to try to pass. They wouldn't dare try that in a bank."

"But why was the phony money hidden here? In Mrs. Browne's purse? Do you think she hid it or had someone else taken it?" Amanda asked.

"That wasn't the purse that was on the bed this morning," Caroline said. "I'm totally confused as to what is going on. But I certainly don't like her hanging about with those three folks."

"They seem harmless enough," Louisa said. "The worse that could happen is your mother might be bored to death with tales of Mother Russia from Mister Rostov or fall into a deep sleep after the umpteenth wearisome historical anecdote. Has he given you the Ambrose Burnside story again?"

"Yes, please don't remind me. Wherever they've gone, I hope they come back soon."

Required to stay at the hotel, most of the party stayed in the lobby chatting, playing cards or reading. The exceptions were the Sheriff, Brendan and Amanda, who continued to go over the details of what they knew so far.

The quiet was disturbed when the front door burst open and a big man in a sturdy coat, boots and a flannel hat with ear flaps glared at them.

"Where in tarnation is Foster!" he shouted to no one in particular.

"Hold on, Mister Carroll," the Sheriff said, getting up and putting himself between the man and access to the office. Both the Fosters had been working but were now on their feet at the disturbance.

"Where is my girl?" he thundered.

The Sheriff was about the same size as the newcomer and stood face to face with him, daring him to back down.

"And all you people playing cards! Not a care in the world! And my girl is missing?"

"We're not sure she's missing. Well, she's not here, but we don't know where she went or with who. Does Olive have a boyfriend?" the Sheriff asked.

"She'd better not! Unless she met some drifter here at the hotel. We've had plenty of arguments about her working here when she could be at home helping her mother and me."

"I'm sure she gives you her wages, though, doesn't she?" the Sheriff asked, knowing it was the custom.

"That's none of your business. When's the last time anyone saw her?"

Eunice had heard the uproar from the kitchen and came out to see what the matter was. "She was last seen in the middle of the night when we were all disturbed by an incident," she said, carefully choosing her words.

"What kind of incident?"

Eunice looked to Greg who shook his head slightly and she didn't respond.

"There was someone going from room to room, checking to see if the doors were locked. We don't know who it was, but by then everyone was awakened," Brendan said, deciding not to mention the attack on Amanda to spare either the man's feelings of anger or fear.

"I went up to see why she was late coming down this morning and saw that she had packed her things," Eunice said.

Mister Carroll took off his hat, his salt-and-pepper hair standing up from the static. "So, nobody knows why she left, when she left or with who."

"I'm afraid not. It's clear she didn't leave on foot."

"Of course not. She may be reckless, but she's not foolhardy enough to try to get anywhere on foot in this weather. Even with a good pair of boots. Lugging a suitcase, too." He slapped his hat against his leg in frustration.

"I've got one of my deputies on the lookout in Pittsfield. That's where she may have gone, but we can't be sure."

"What can I do?" the father asked.

"We're going to have lunch soon," Eunice said. "You may as well take off your coat and have something to eat while we wait to hear some news."

He scowled at her but took off his coat and hat and looked around for a coatrack on which to place them. "After that, unless my wife calls with news and if she hasn't come back, I'm going into town to look for her myself," he said.

"I think we're all going to participate in the hunt."

Humbled by Mister Carroll's distress, the guests had ceased playing cards and sat quietly. Caroline introduced herself and mentioned that her mother was missing as well.

"What? Two women missing? We're not that far from the Canadian border," he said.

Amanda gave Caroline a stern look to suggest that she had not made the situation better with her information about her mother.

"I'm sorry. I should clarify. My mother went into town without telling me or anybody. And the Sheriff was very specific that everyone should stay here until things got sorted out."

Jimmy's large frame appeared at the end of the hallway in his chef's attire. "It's a bit early, but lunch is served," he said, disappearing back to the kitchen.

"I can't say I'm particularly hungry, but we may as well eat while we can," Amanda said to Brendan.

They filed into the dining room with the Sheriff and Caroline sitting with the silent Mister Carroll, who had never eaten there before. Eunice was assisted by Jimmy in bringing out the bowls of stew and biscuits, a one-bowl meal to reduce the need for table service. The room was quiet as the soup spoons clanked against the bowls, interrupted only by the occasional, "Pass the butter, please."

They ate in silence for some time until they heard loud voices from the lobby and Mister Carroll got up abruptly to see if it was Olive. Instead, he was confronted by Hextilda, red-cheeked with her hair sticking out at angles from the knitted cap she wore.

"Hello, who are you?" she could be heard to ask cheerily.

"Who in tarnation are you?"

"Hextilda Browne," she said holding out her hand.

Caroline came barreling into the lobby from the dining room. "Mother! Where have you been? I've been worried sick!"

"Why? I just went into town with the Dalrymples and Mister Rostov."

"You weren't supposed to leave, remember? And where are they?" she asked, looking over her mother's shoulder toward the front drive, expecting to see the Dalrymple car or the other passengers.

"They've stayed in town to take care of some things. Mr. Rostov wanted to check in with the doctor again. I hired a car to bring me back."

"Have you seen my daughter, Olive?" Mister Carroll asked her.

"Who's that?"

"She works here."

"Why, no. Not today at least."

"What business did you have to attend to that was so urgent?" Caroline asked.

"I'll tell you all about it after I freshen up."

"Lunch has already been served. Come into the dining room and have something to eat first. Then tell me what is going on."

All three went to the dining room and the other guests gaped at the sight of the oblivious Mrs. Browne smiling and waving at them as if nothing were the matter. She was aware that nobody was smiling back, least of all the Sheriff, who glowered at her. He decided to wait after everyone was finished eating before he confronted her.

"Things in town are certainly lively as everyone seems to have the Christmas spirit," she said. "Biscuits! Oh, I love biscuits. I must tell Mister Foster what a wonderful chef he has, making all the basic, homestyle foods that go so well when you're in the wilderness."

Mister Carroll stared at her. "My daughter Olive is missing," he stated.

"I'm sorry. I didn't know."

"Eat up, Mother. I'm sure the Sheriff wants to talk to you about your companions, where you've been and another interesting matter."

"That sounds exciting," she said, digging into the stew.

The meal over, the Sheriff, Brendan, Amanda and Caroline took Mrs. Browne into the library to quiz her on the morning's activities.

Rob and Louisa were seated in the far corner across a small table from John and Aggie, who were about to start a rubber of bridge. They stood to leave, but the Sheriff waved them back down.

"All of us might as well hear everything," he said, resigned to some obfuscation from Mrs. Browne.

"Mother, why did you leave when the Sheriff asked us not to?" Caroline asked.

"I told you I had some business to attend to."

Seeing she was not going to get a straight answer, she asked, "Why did you have all that money in your handbag this morning."

Hextilda's eyes widened, but she said nothing.

Caroline snatched the handbag from her mother's grip and opening it to the others in the room said, "And now it's not here."

Mrs. Browne took it back, summoning her dignity. "It's none of your business."

"I think it is. And I think your new friends have something to do with it, don't they?"

"The Dalrymples have nothing to do with it. Well, almost nothing."

"I'm talking about Mister Rostov."

Hextilda didn't meet her daughter's glare.

"Well, tell us!"

"The Dalrymples said they wanted to stay in town for the night. We dropped Mister Rostov off at the doctor's office first."

"Excuse me, but what doctor?" John asked from across the room.

"Thomas. No, Thompson. Nice looking gentleman. His office is in this professional building on the main street," she said.

"I have an office in that building. And there is no Doctor Thompson in Pittsfield."

"I may have got his name wrong or something. We had taken Mister Rostov to him just yesterday. I saw the name on the door." Hextilda was perplexed. "I don't understand."

"What was the money for, Mother?"

Hextilda twisted her hands in her lap. "It was a charitable donation."

"To whom?"

"For a humanitarian cause."

"How much?"

Hextilda had stalled as much as possible before blurting the amount. "Five thousand dollars."

Caroline's eyes widened at the sum. "For what exactly?"

Gathering her courage, Hextilda began her story. "As you may know, or perhaps not, Mister Rostov fled Russia after the Revolution as a relatively young man. He told me a heart-breaking story of his family escaping to the countryside, leaving all their city property behind and taking the bare minimum with them. When even the rural areas became unsafe, they left again and came to Europe, and after the death of his parents, who were broken by the experience, he came to America."

"Was the money for him?"

"No, he had been on a fundraising tour and came to Boston. He feared for his life and that is why we came here to discuss the issue further. The rescue, you see."

"You said his parents were dead. Who were you trying to rescue?"

"Why, the Grand Duchess Anastasia, of course," her mother said with irritation.

"But she perished long ago," Brendan said.

"That's what everyone thinks, and her supporters encourage that belief. In fact, she is alive in Russia under an assumed name. What she needs are funds to bribe one official or another and get a passport and means to travel out of the country."

The room was silent.

"The Spanish Prisoner," Rob said from the other side of the room.

"What? No. She's not in Spain, she's in Russia somewhere."

"It's not a location. It's the name of a confidence scheme," Rob said, standing up. "Someone approaches the 'mark,' apologies, Mrs. Browne, and tells a heartbreaking story of someone being held hostage or against their will. That person needs to be rescued and what they need above all are the funds to make it happen."

The room was silent as the pieces fell into place.

"It's what they call a 'con' for confidence game. My guess is after telling this terrible story of woe and suffering, Mister Rostov claimed he was giving what little he had left to the cause and asked you to hold it for him."

"Why, yes! That's how I knew he was sincere," Hextilda said. "And the Dalrymples pledged a like amount once they got back to the bank."

"The money he gave you was counterfeit," the Sheriff said. "His money was worthless and the money you took from your account at the bank was authentic."

Hextilda put her hands up to her face. "That's not possible," she said in a whisper, not wanting to believe what she was being told. "Oh! The Dalrymples! If this is true, you must warn them! They'll be impoverished by this—and him a private school teacher!"

"It seems Professor Dalrymple is neither a professor nor a teacher at that school. We checked."

"I don't understand." Hextilda said.

"What don't you understand, Mother? You've been swindled. And just lost five thousand dollars."

"But…"

"The money he gave you to trust his investment was counterfeit. We found it upstairs."

There was silence for a few minutes as everyone took in the information presented. Caroline relented and sat next to her mother and embraced her.

"So, who hit me on the head? And why?" Amanda asked.

"I suspect it was Dalrymple or whatever his name is. We may find out if we ever find those folks."

"What do we do now?" Caroline asked.

"It's time to go into Pittsfield and track them down. If

they've got your money, they'll be leaving town as quickly as possible."

"What does this have to do with Tony, the porter?"

"I suspect he either recognized these folks from some other place or overheard a conversation they were having. He had to be silenced," the Sheriff said. "Let's take as many cars as we need. Don't anyone go off on their own to confront these people.

Chapter 20

Rob took his car with Louisa, Brendan and Amanda while John and Aggie were together in theirs with Hextilda and Caroline. The Sheriff had his own vehicle, as did Olive's father. They reasoned that among them, they could track down the miscreants and possibly retrieve the money.

It was a race into Pittsfield and as they entered town, the Sheriff flagged down his deputy to ask for any updates on Olive or the Dalrymples.

"I saw a few New York plates," the officer responded. "I called over to Albany to see who the car was registered to, but it turns out it was stolen a few days ago."

The doddering Professor and his wife were more nefarious than the Sheriff had imagined.

He stopped in front of the Pittsfield Hotel, thinking the couple may have intended to spend the night there.

"Do you have a couple named Dalrymple who registered?"

he asked the desk clerk without preamble since everyone knew he was the Sheriff.

"No. No couple has registered today."

"May I look at your register?"

"Sure. What's up?" the young man behind the desk asked.

"Do you know an Olive Carroll? Has she checked in?"

"I don't know her, and nobody by that name has checked in."

"Who's this Audrey Wilson?"

"She checked in earlier today. Just spending the night and leaving tomorrow."

"Give me the key," the Sheriff said, holding out his hand.

The clerk did as he was told, and the Sheriff took the stairs by twos to get up to the next floor. He pounded on the door and heard a quiet voice ask who was there.

"It's the Sheriff, Olive," he said. "Open up and if you don't, I've got a key."

The door was unlocked, and Olive peered out at the Sheriff's grim face.

"What are you doing here?" she asked him.

"I was about to ask the same thing of you," he said pushing his way into the room.

"I've left my job at the Mountain Aire. I got a better position in Albany, if you must know."

"With who? The Dalrymples?"

Olive smiled. "That's not his real name and he's not a professor or teacher even. He's an agent working for the FBI."

"What?"

"He's been tracking down this kidnap plot that involved Tony and since he's dead now, he needs some help with the further investigation. He's hired me to help him."

The Sheriff stared at her. "How, exactly?"

"I think he wants me to be like an assistant investigator. I think it's very exciting."

"Where are he and his wife now?"

"Getting the car ready to drive back to New York."

"You'd better get your things together immediately. I believe you may have been tricked into this," the Sheriff said. He pulled her suitcase from the closet, opened it and said, "Put everything in here. Now."

She went to the bathroom and got whatever toiletries she had put there, then opened the chest of drawers and while deciding how to take out her clothes, the Sheriff grabbed the lot and threw them into the case.

"Your father is waiting downstairs. Come with me."

Olive only had time to grab her coat and hat before scurrying to catch up to the Sheriff going down the stairs into the lobby carrying her suitcase with one stocking hanging out the side.

"Sir, sir!" the clerk said. "The bill! Nobody has paid for the room yet!"

The Sheriff ignored him and propelled Olive to her father's vehicle.

Mister Carroll put aside his feelings of relief in order to scold her, "You almost killed your mother with worry." She burst into tears at the reprimand and the lost opportunity of working for the Dalrymples.

The Sheriff went over to Rob's car and relayed the information that three tricksters were driving their car out of town headed either east to Boston, west to Albany or south to New York.

"What do you recommend?" Rob asked, ready to participate in a car chase, if that's what it took.

While he was making up his mind how to proceed, his deputy pulled up.

"That car with the New York plates hit a telephone pole up the road."

"Where are the occupants?" the Sheriff asked, ready to sprint to his car.

"Someone saw it and said only a young man was in the car and he jogged back into town."

Brendan and the Sheriff looked at each other.

"Jogged? Can't be Rostov and I can't imagine Dalrymple running," Brendan said.

"Let's go to the Professional Building and see the 'doctor' that was treating Rostov. He has to be in on this, too."

The Carrolls turned around and headed back for the farm while the three cars continued to the building where John

Taylor had his office and where Hextilda had gone with Rostov and the Dalrymples just the day before.

They pulled up outside and decided that only Hextilda should come with them to show them the room, but Caroline insisted on accompanying her mother and Amanda was not going to be left out of the investigation. They went to the third floor and Hextilda marched confidently ahead of them.

"See? Doctor Thompson," she pointed at the lettering on the frosted glass of the door.

The Sheriff tried the door and found it unlocked. Turning on the lights, they beheld the chaos of clothing strewn across the room.

"That's the exam room," she said, and Brendan opened the door to find a table with a cloth on it, nothing more.

"It can't be!" she said.

"Look!" Amanda said, pawing through the mess of clothing. "That drab brown coat that Mrs. Dalrymple wore. And her tweeds."

"And what's this? A false beard? And a gray wig?" the Sheriff asked. "Is that a set of false teeth?"

They stood looking at the pile of discarded clothes before Hextilda gasped. "His cast! The doctor must have cut it off him!"

"My guess is that the cast was a prop that he could take off at will. And I'll bet you he may have been the shadowy figure in the dark that hit me on the head," Amanda said.

"Or the supposed doctor. Whoever that person was."

There was another door which, when opened, revealed a closet with hangers partially on the rod with others on the floor.

"They certainly left in a hurry."

"But how? They no longer have a car."

"They might be headed to the train station," the Sheriff said. He looked at his watch. "The train to Boston leaves in about fifteen minutes."

They raced out of the room and to the elevator, leaving Hextilda and Caroline to catch up if they could. The doors to the elevator closed as they called out, "Wait for us!"

"Don't worry, they can catch a ride with John and Aggie," Amanda said.

The Sheriff ran to his car while Brendan and Amanda went to Rob's.

"What in the world is going on?" Louisa said.

"The Dalrymples were in full disguise. Fake beard for the Professor and a wig for the missus," Amanda said.

"Thank goodness that wasn't her real hair. It was dreadful."

Amanda looked at her sister and had to laugh. "You'll be pleased to know she left the tweeds and the brown overcoat behind, too. Oh, and there was a discarded cast on the floor next to those ghastly plus fours and argyle socks."

"Very clever of them to at once look so dowdy and on the other hand so loud that nobody was paying attention to what was really going on."

Just as Rob was putting the car in gear, John and Aggie pulled up next to them.

"Where to now?" he asked.

"Let's follow the Sheriff to the train station. Could you wait for Caroline and Mrs. Browne? We don't have room for them." Rob pulled forward but caught the look of irritation on John's face.

"We always get to do the dirty work," he grumbled to Aggie.

"Hurry up," she urged the two women, who looked dazed as they exited the building.

The three cars pulled up to the station's parking area where two taxis stood waiting. The Sheriff looked briefly in each one, but seeing nobody in the back, dashed into the station, followed by Brendan. One customer was just finishing the purchase of a ticket when the Sheriff pushed past him and asked the clerk, "Have you seen four people—strangers, three men and a woman—who bought tickets to Boston?"

"No, I don't reckon I did. But you can check if you want," he gestured to the waiting train and the Sheriff and Brendan got on and ran through the first car, excusing themselves as they bumped into people rearranging their luggage.

"They may have split up," Brendan said. "We need to look carefully at their faces."

They slowed down in the second car where only a handful of people sat, one man with a newspaper held up to his face.

"Excuse me, sir," he said, pulling the paper down to get a look at his face.

"I beg your pardon!"

They made sure to look in the washrooms at the end of each car in the event the scoundrels were hiding there.

Another man was lounging in a seat with a hat over his eyes. The Sheriff lifted it up to the man's surprise and then continued to the third car. Neither that car nor the last had many passengers, and none that were the Dalrymples, Rostov or the doctor, although they did not have a good description of the latter.

The whistle blew, indicating the train would soon be leaving, and they raced to the door and jumped down to the platform.

"Do you think they may have rented a car or a driver?" Brendan asked.

"There are drivers for hire, yes, but it would be pricey to commission a ride to Boston or New York. However, I wouldn't put it past them to stiff the driver once they got where they were going."

"What now?"

"That's the last train for the day. But maybe they went to the bus station. The express buses have left but there are locals that take much longer to get to Boston."

"Where's that station?"

"Other side of town," the Sheriff said.

John had pulled up in the meantime and put his head out the window. "Where are we going now?"

"Bus," Brendan answered, and John sped off, knowing his way around town. He was followed by the Sheriff and Rob's full car.

"This is so exciting," Louisa said.

Amanda leaned forward from the back seat. "One of them shot the porter, so they may be armed. I would contain my excitement, if I were you, and hunker down in the seat."

Rob patted her arm. "We'll be okay. These folks are grifters first and foremost. They're in it for the money, not to cause mayhem."

"Except they already have," Brendan said.

The other side of town turned out to be less than a ten-minute drive in the dark as the streetlights came on.

"Do you really think these folks would take a bus?" Louisa asked.

"They knew the car was hot and didn't dare travel far in it. I suspect the telephone pole accident was done on purpose to deflect attention from their other misdeeds. Maybe we're supposed to think that they are still in town and waste time searching hotels and guest houses," Brendan said.

They arrived at the bus station and saw a small stream of people coming out the front door.

"What's all this traffic?" Brendan asked the Sheriff as they left their cars.

"The local folks who work nearby use it to get to the coat factory and papermill. Shifts for both ended about forty minutes ago. And these people? Most papermill men and women on the next shift," he said.

They scanned the room and Brendan felt something at his back. It was Amanda's hand.

"What are you doing in here?" he scowled at her. "You should have stayed in the car."

"I bet I'll spot them before you do," she said.

"The three men could be dressed down to look like mill workers," the Sheriff said. "I'm going outside and see if anybody has got on the bus yet."

There was only the driver behind the wheel, looking toward the waiting room.

"Hey, Sheriff! What's going on?" he asked with a smile.

"Never mind, Ben. Just looking for someone."

"Dangerous?" the driver asked.

"Could be."

The smile was wiped off Ben's face. "Armed?" he asked in a whisper.

"Don't know. But you may want to close the door and not let anyone in just yet. We wouldn't want these folks to hijack your bus."

The driver did as he was told, and the Sheriff went back to the waiting room, scanning the crowd. He saw people he knew and some he didn't. Those he didn't recognize got extra scrutiny.

Amanda had gone to the woman's restroom to wash her hands and observed a smart pair of shoes under one of the stalls. It didn't look like something a mill worker would wear. She dried her hands and made a loud business of opening and closing the door to the waiting room although she remained inside. A few moments later, an elegant woman with a stylish hat and coat emerged from one of the stalls and went to the sink to wash her hands. It wasn't until she reached for the towel that she saw Amanda.

"Mrs. Dalrymple! What a swanky outfit."

The woman, fully made up and looking twenty years younger than her former self, glared at her, then tried to push past to open the door and, in doing so, knocked Amanda to the floor in front of the door, blocking her escape.

"Help! Brendan! Help! We've got her!" she screamed.

Amanda saw that the elegant shoe with its silk stocking was about to kick her in the face and instead, she grabbed the leg and pulled the woman sharply to the floor. She yelped and let out colorful language while they continued to grapple on the tile flooring.

The door opened and Brendan came in and pulled Amanda to her feet before grabbing the fake Mrs. Dalrymple up gruffly.

"Where's the old man and your partners."

"Figure it out, copper," she sneered.

They didn't have to figure it out. By the time they exited the bathroom, the Sheriff had spotted Rostov, who was slouched in the corner trying to make himself invisible with the fake Professor, also looking years younger, clean shaven and in stylish clothes, reading a magazine. John Taylor had entered the building at that point and assisted the Sheriff in detaining the men.

"Where's the doc?" the Sheriff asked. He didn't need to because at that moment a young man was pushing his way out of the waiting room to the bus only to find the door closed. Pounding on the bus door did not result in his admittance and he froze when he saw the imposing figure or John coming his way.

"Fellow medical colleague, are you?" John asked and pulled the young man's arm behind his back and frog-marched him into the waiting room.

The Sheriff had already asked the clerk to telephone for the deputy to come assist as there were four people to be detained and not much room in the cars at the scene. It was quite a sight for the workers going on shift, and they murmured among themselves as to what variety of bandits had come to Pittsfield to cause such a stir.

"Well, these factory folks are safe," the Sheriff said. "The wages they make aren't worth being swindled out of."

The Sheriff made sure to frisk each of the four to check for weapons, came up cold but pulled a passport out of Rostov's suit pocket. He opened it and showed it to Brendan.

"Albert Carmichael?" Brendan asked.

"It's as good a name as any," the former Rostov said in an American accent.

"And look. Recently in Canada. I think we've found our connection," the Sheriff said.

They trooped outside where Hextilda and Caroline stood, their eyes wide at the different appearance of the four collaborators.

"Martha is so much younger than I thought," Hextilda said.

"Mother, I'm sure that is not her real name. And as we discovered, she doesn't have gray hair, wear glasses or have buckteeth since we saw them on the floor back in the bogus doctor's office."

As the former Mrs. Dalrymple passed by, Hextilda snatched the woman's purse and, turning, opened it quickly.

"Hey!" the woman yelled. "Get your mitts off that!"

Hextilda held up an envelope and yelped in triumph. "My money!"

Caroline reached up and took the envelope from her mother. "Let me be the guardian of this, if you don't mind."

"I certainly do mind," her mother said, but Caroline pulled it behind her back.

"From now on, I think I should insert myself more into the family's finances. We can't afford to have something like this happen again."

"I protest!"

"Fred and I will work on that together. I have long had the suspicion that your self-proclaimed renown as an author has not been verified by the income."

Hextilda was furious and clamped her lips together. But, for once, she had nothing to say.

Chapter 21

The Sheriff took his prisoners to the county jail with the assistance of his deputy while the others made their way back to the Mountain Aire. Brendan asked George to join them in the lobby along with Greg, Jimmy and Eunice.

"And in celebration, let's have a round of cocktails," Caroline suggested.

Hextilda, who had been in a dark mood since being humiliated at the bus station, brightened up immediately. "Hear, hear!"

She sank into one of the sofas and looked at Rob, the nearest male. "Do put more wood on the fire, won't you? I'm still chilled from our expedition."

Rob smiled and did as she asked, adding a large log for what might be a long evening.

When the drinks arrived and everyone was seated, Brendan held up his glass in a toast.

"Here's to an end of a puzzling investigation," he said.

"Wait—but who killed Tony and why?" Eunice asked.

"We have the solution to one part of the scheme. And it does connect to Tony. Rostov, also known as Albert Carmichael, probably among other names, and the Dalrymples, whose real names we don't yet know, and a younger man posing as a doctor were all part of a clever and well executed con. It's called a con because the person or persons who instigate it earn the confidence of the mark," and here he nodded at Hextilda, who cringed at being so labeled. "They do so with stories of suffering and possible rescue of someone in need. In this case, it was the Grand Duchess Anastasia, who some people believe is still alive. After filling Mrs. Browne's head with the hardships the poor deposed woman had borne over the years, he suggested that she could assist in getting her out of Russia where she had been in hiding for these long years. Money was needed to bribe officials, get false documents, arrange travel to the United States where she would be greeted with open arms by the émigré community. And, of course, be eternally grateful to the generous Mrs. Browne."

Hextilda was looking into her martini glass although absorbing every word.

"Rostov had already been in touch with your mother in Boston through her large social network and he persuaded her to meet him here because he said he feared for his safety. That coincided nicely with the kidnap scheme that her man Bannister had cooked up and was a good excuse to leave town. Influenced by Rostov's comments about danger combined with what she had imagined was going to happen to her daughter, she gladly agreed."

"Did you think Tony was a danger to you?" Eunice asked Hextilda.

"I'm not sure. He startled me on more than one occasion and his accented English made me suspicious of his intentions."

"Did you shoot him?" Eunice asked, standing up. "You were here in the hotel while we went into town. You could have come downstairs to get something to eat in the kitchen, been startled by him again and, frightened, pulled the trigger."

"No, no. I certainly did not!" Hextilda said.

"And what about Caroline? She came back early from skiing because of an imagined muscle problem. She could have got her mother's gun and, suspecting that Tony was one of the kidnappers, shot him before wiping off her fingerprints and dashing upstairs to be with her mother as her alibi and cover," Eunice said.

"What about you?" Caroline said, standing. "Olive loved to gossip, and she told me you were sweet on Tony and hoped to get away from your loveless marriage with him. You could have stolen the gun my mother had bragged about from her handbag. Were you planning on killing your husband?"

"How dare you?" Eunice yelled.

"But Tony was more interested in Olive and once you told him of your plan and he told you about his relationship with Olive, you killed him," Caroline said.

"Please, please. Sit down. Calm down. You've got it all wrong," Brendan said.

Caroline and Eunice sat but continued to glare at one another.

"It has nothing to do with love," Brendan said. "Real or imagined."

The assembled group shifted anxiously in their chairs, awaiting the real explanation.

Brendan took another sip of his martini and resumed.

"Rostov thought that the Berkshires were obscure enough that nobody would recognize him. He enlisted the couple we all knew as the Dalrymples to meet him here although pretending not to know him. They pulled off their disguises by pretending to be obtuse, oblivious and boring so nobody paid them much attention. Rostov had the leg cast made some time ago, I think, and that and the crutches were a perfect way to attract attention to his disability and, on the other hand, to discount his ability to move quickly, if at all."

"What he hadn't counted on was Tony Rivers working as a porter and waiter here. Tony must have seen through his disguise and remembered him and the other couple from when he worked in Canada, where hotel guests were fleeced in a confidence scheme very like the one that was perpetrated here. He wasn't sure but looked through Rostov's room when we were all at dinner and discovered enough to confirm that he was right. However, he didn't confront Rostov until the next day when we were skiing, the staff went to town and Tony stayed. Why? I believe to challenge Rostov and possibly get some of the gains from the scam. Rostov had already suspected that Tony recognized him and the previous night, when he heard Hextilda bragging about having brought a gun, he waited until she was at breakfast the next morning to steal it. Remember, he didn't have to clomp along slowly with crutches but once unencumbered by the easily removed cast, was able to move swiftly. All that was left was to wait until everyone was gone and Hextilda was alone in her room with some malady, then to go downstairs and ascertain what Tony knew or didn't know."

"We may never know what that conversation was about. It's likely that Tony acknowledged that Rostov was the same man who engineered a con game in the hotel in Canada. Did he threaten Rostov? Or did he want a cut of the action?"

"He would never," Eunice said. "He was an honest man."

Greg looked at her in astonishment. She looked down into her lap, embarrassed by her outburst.

Amanda picked up the thread. "He had already got an accomplice to rent a vacant space in the Professional Building, got a name painted on the door and with minimal props —some chairs, a table and a doctor's coat—they were able to persuade Mrs. Browne that Rostov's broken leg was indeed real and foster more sympathy for the man. Then, they went to the bank where he led her to believe he had extracted money from an account. They went to the restaurant where he made his pitch. Part of that was probably asking her to hold the money he had taken out for safekeeping to build trust that he was an honest man. Little did she know that the money he had her hold was counterfeit. It wasn't withdrawn from the bank; he already had it in his suit pocket. By mistake, one of the bills was still in his pocket and he paid for the luncheon bill with it, which the owner recognized as fake and later reported to the police and in turn the Sheriff."

"The Dalrymples were also at the luncheon and they, too, probably pledged to give funds for the rescue of the Grand

Duchess. Of course, that was just to bolster Mrs. Browne's trust in the scheme. After lunch, they went back to the bank where the Dalrymples pretended to withdraw whatever they had promised, and Mrs. Browne did the same. However, hers was the only real money in the game. The rest was counterfeit or just paper in an envelope meant to look like a wad of cash."

Hextilda closed her eyes and exhaled.

Brendan took up the narrative. "But Rostov wanted to distract anyone who was already jittery after the murder of Tony in the hopes that they would all leave, putting an end to the investigation. He pulled the stunt of trying everyone's door in the middle of the night, not actually expecting someone would come out into the corridor to check. Alas, Amanda was that curious person who was struck on the head for her trouble and Rostov was able to run back to his room, put the cast back on and hobble out when the hue and cry went up."

"Everyone was on edge and Olive told the Dalrymples that she had seen someone in the hall, but didn't know who it was. They sympathized with her about being afraid and said that they were leaving the next day and could rescue her from the dangerous situation if she got her things together right then. They couldn't chance that she had figured out who it was. She readily agreed to the suggestion and Mr. Dalrymple drove her into Pittsfield in the dark where she registered as Audrey something-or-other and was to wait for the next day when they would take her back with them to Albany. And there she waited until late in the day when we discovered her, and her father hauled her back to the farm."

"At some point, Rostov and the Dalrymples met back at the Professional Building, where they had ample time to rid themselves of the disguises and then just wait until dark to leave town. The accomplice was probably supposed to leave the car parked somewhere but it ended up in a telephone pole, either intentionally or by mistake. Dark came and they went to the bus station looking like four well-to-do people as they bought their tickets. With real money, of course. Rostov had put the counterfeit stuff in a bag he took from Mrs. Browne's room. He wouldn't have wanted to arouse suspicion or guilt if it was found on him. We caught up with them at the bus station after having checked the train station to see they were not on the last train out."

"Where are they now?" Gordon asked.

"The county jail, I understand."

"What about the Grand Duchess?" Hextilda asked.

"Oh, Mother. Really!" Caroline sputtered. "Get a clue! I think it's time we went home."

"Are we free to go?" her mother asked Brendan.

"I think so. You may be called back here when these folks go to trial, but that's down the road."

"You'll know where to find me. It's the house in Beacon Hill where the greatest fool in Boston lives." She left with her daughter and the staff cleared the empty glasses, leaving only the three couples in the lobby.

"What shall we do? We haven't had much time for skiing," Amanda asked Brendan.

"Rob, Louisa—what do you want to do?"

"I, for one, am done with this place," Louisa said. "I couldn't bear to spend another day here."

"It doesn't make sense to go skiing tomorrow and then drive home. We'll all be tired from the exercise," Rob said.

"I've got to check in on some patients at the hospital," John said. "Why don't you all come back to West Adams for dinner and to stay the night?"

"The beds are still made up," Aggie added.

They could hear an argument going on in the kitchen.

Amanda lowered her voice. "I think that is our cue to leave."

"It's just as well. I hope to never see Hextilda Browne again," Louisa said.

Amanda had to laugh. "After this, you know that she will have to save face and reconsider striking us off the guest list for Fred and Valerie's wedding in February."

"Oh, no. Well, I'll consider it a mandatory party. What could be so bad?"

The Burnside sisters and Brendan will soon discover what that might be in:
MURDER AT THE VALENTINE WEDDING
Reviews help readers discover my books, so feel free to leave a comment on my
REVIEW PAGE
For more updates, check out my newsletter:
www.Andreas-books.com